the OBSECRATION

Broken Eye Books is an independent press, here to bring you the odd, strange, and offbeat side of speculative fiction. Our stories tend to blend genres, highlighting the weird and blurring its boundaries with horror, sci-fi, and fantasy.

Support weird. Support indie.

brokeneyebooks.com
twitter.com/brokeneyebooks
facebook.com/brokeneyebooks
instagram.com/brokeneyebooks

"Matthew M. Bartlett is the mad prince of weird fiction. Welcome to Leeds." (**Paul Tremblay**, author of *A Head Full of Ghosts* and *The Cabin at the End of the World*)

"Not all writers are storytellers, but Matthew M. Bartlett sure is. *The Obsecration* will draw you in with its first unsettling sentence and hold you rapt and breathless until its last unnerving image." (**Molly Tanzer**, author of *Creatures of Will and Temper* and *Vermilion*)

"Bartlett writes like a man in the grip of a vision, when he writes like a man at all and not just a pile of worms in a man-shaped suit." (**Orrin Grey**, author of *How to See Ghosts & Other Figments*)

"A new book by Matthew M. Bartlett is always cause for celebration. Bartlett is a sui generis figure in modern horror fiction—there's no one quite like him. Most writers, whether by design or not, fall into categories or factions or frameworks built by the giants of the genre, but Bartlett stands in no one's shadow. He's a species all his own, brilliant and terrifying and unique, and when the cartographers of the Weird map the horror-lit scene of the twenty-first century, Matthew M. Bartlett's work will stand alone." (**Polly Schattel**, author of *Shadowdays* and *The Occultists*)

"In Matthew M. Bartlett's splendid *The Obsecration*, the apocalypse comes to the town of Leeds, Massachusetts. All of the ingredients of a 1980s-style horror blockbuster are here: a small town setting, multiple points of view, a cast of outsiders, a sinister henchman, a malevolent villain whose return threatens the end of everything. Bartlett boils them down to a thick broth of Grand Guignol gore, psychological disintegration, and cosmic nihilism. Familiar elements of his fiction—WXXT, malevolent corporations, ventriloquist's dummies, those awful flying leeches—swim in the mix, together with new disturbances. Hieronymus Bosch, Lucio Fulci, Thomas Ligotti, and Stephen King are just some of the apostles elbowing for position around the table, but at its center sits Matthew Bartlett, his head surrounded by a halo of flies." (**John Langan**, author of *Corpsemouth and Other Autobiographies*)

the OBSECRATION

THE OBSECRATION
by MATTHEW M. BARTLETT

Published by
Broken Eye Books
www.brokeneyebooks.com

978-1-940372-70-9 (trade paperback)
978-1-940372-71-6 (hardcover)

the OBSECRATION

Matthew M. Bartlett

Who Beareth the Body

THE LOOK DINER HUNKERS LOW AT THE FAR END OF THE LOT BY THE TREE line, like a creature with its belly to the ground, preparing to pounce. In the orange-yellow panorama of booth-lined windows, silhouettes sit alone or in pairs. The sun, having been bullied back by clouds for the length of the afternoon, has given up and ducked behind the horizon to cower and heal. To the west, on Roaring Spring Road, cars with glowing eyes slide through the blue dusk. To the north, the movie marquee that flanks the access road shouts non sequiturs at indifferent commuters.

Follow me now down the walk littered with curled-up cigarette butts and discarded pennies, past the newspaper boxes with their cracked plastic windows, past the ransacked phone booth graffitied with peeled and faded stickers. Follow me through the front door into the carpeted vestibule with its gumball and decal machines and its particle-board rack of unread pamphlets and flyers. I pull open the interior doors, and we are greeted with a breeze redolent of bacon and burnt butter and overcooked beef. The colors are rust and umber, yellow tile speckled brown. The host's podium stands vacant, a lectern bereft of its lector.

A polite sign tells us, PLEASE SEAT YOURSELVES. So let's grab the big booth in the corner, the one with the round table and the crescent-shaped seat. Though we are only two, the table might easily fit six—seven if the seventh grabs a chair—and if it's Lucy's shift and her table, she won't mind. The crumbs and water rings have been whisked and wiped away, and the surface of the table still shines, the swirling contours left by the dampened cloth fading even as we approach. The view will be best from here.

Why are we at the Look Diner tonight? It's not for the tepid coffee or the waffles straight from the freezer, not for the overcooked beef and the butter-sotted toast. No. We are here because something is going to happen tonight.

Look, but don't get caught looking. Make like you're eyeing the tall blonde, settling her bill over at the cash register. Or perusing the freestanding sign with its list of uninspired specials written in multicolored neon on black, spangled with five-pointed stars and unnecessary apostrophes. Now let your glance slide over to the fat man at the centermost round table. His flabby belly hangs low between his thighs. Watch as he bends his neck, his white beard folding into an *L*, to peruse the menu, syrup-splotched and gilded along one side with a stretched-out teardrop of coagulated yolk. Propped up against his chair is his gnarled wooden cane, a silent confidant, a bulge-fisted familiar. The man's chewed, dirt-lined pinky nail underlines the list of side orders line by line as his lips mouth the words, buffeting his mustache with halitosis-freighted wind.

The door dings, and two women—a bleached blonde and a dyed-too-black brunette, all long bare legs and teased hair—waft in on a wave of perfume and tobacco smoke. They whisper and titter as they bypass the podium, plopping down on either side of the bearded man. The brunette rests the crook of her high heel on the edge of the table, her black shorts sliding up to reveal the moon-white curve of a buttock and a pink-splotched thigh crinkled with cellulite. The three converse in hushed tones as a waitress rushes over with two menus and silverware enshrouded in napkins.

Jake, the slender, acne-scarred busboy, peers out under the awning of pale-green guest checks.

"Behind you," chirps Marci, bumping his backside with her prodigious hip as she sweeps by, holding aloft a round tray teeming with milkshake-stained glasses and plates caked with crusts and carnage and strips of fat.

Jake grunts a reply. Marci deposits the tray and swings back his way. She thrusts her face next to his, her warm ear grazing his. He winces at her excessive perfume, cloying, like plums just gone over. "Strippers," she says. "Excuse me.

Exotic dancers. They wriggle around on guys' hard-ons at the Whateley Ballet for a couple soggy dollars. But you probably already know that."

"Behind you," says Shantaya as she pushes past the two, a greasy cloth in one hand and in the other . . . well, how strange. For just a moment, it looks like she's gripping by the neck a catatonic cassowary with a red wattle and panicked eyes. At second glance though, it's simply a dark spray bottle with a red trigger. Wipe your eyes, dig at the corners, but you can't wipe away the surety: it was a bird, and now it's a bottle.

Standing at the griddle, a white-coiffed man hewn of oil, spit, and spindle is engaged in a staring contest with the bubbling Argus eyes of a dozen eggs, above which silver-dollar pancakes sit like thought bubbles. He flips the pancakes one by one, the veins shifting under the skin of his wiry arms, his eyes never leaving the eggs. It happens then. Two of the eggs . . . *blink.* A shimmering caul forms at the top edge and slides over the surface of each egg, briefly obscuring the yolks. They retract, and two blood-veined yellow eyes stare up at him before popping apart audibly, droplets of blood springing into the air like water on the surface of a storm-shaken lake. He looks left, looks right. No one is watching. He flips the eggs into the trash barrel and cracks two more. The blood that remains on the griddle he scrapes to the far edge. He flips ten eggs, waits for the latecomers to cook. The surface of the griddle begins to expand and contract. It is a breathing thing. He closes his eyes and waits for it to pass. He opens his eyes, and it's blessedly back to normal.

He puts his back to the grill and scans the dining room.

Everyone is here. If it's going to happen, it's going to happen soon.

Decades, centuries, eons. Nothingness eternal. No one floated in nothingness. His awareness of his own nascent being blossomed slowly. It came to fruition at no time, at which nonpoint it raised up no arms to find its head and found nothing. It moved the no-arms lower to locate its hips and found none. Its no-hands passed through nothing. Nothing moving through nothing. The ghost of a ghost of a ghost of nihil. Decades, centuries, eons. Nothingness eternal.

Abrecan Geist and the Hilltown
Ten : an oral history /
by Anne Gare, et al. -- 1st ed. --
Leeds : Gare Occult, c1961.

(from the introduction by occult historian Michelet Hart)

Parentage and ancestry be damned. To identify the point at which a being slides
bloodily into the world is, at the risk of stating the appallingly obvious, a basic
task of any biographer whose subject is reasonably (even if only regionally)
well-known. In *The Witch-Cult in Western Massachusetts*, a slim compendium
of hastily sketched biographies authored by Anne Gare under a pseudonym,
the brief passage on Geist—suspected to actually have been penned by the
dark mystic himself—indicates a birth year of 1622. We place Geist's birth
just over 250 years later. This distortion is part of a pattern of misinformation
and prevarication peppered throughout his autobiographical writings and
journals, borne of a strong desire to thwart biographers and historians and to
perpetuate a kind of mythology about himself. He often wrote his diaries in the
third person and enhanced them with leaps of fancy, ranging from negligible
exaggerations to full-blown fictions.

You will see in the following pages that longevity—preternatural and
otherwise—is an abiding obsession of Geist's.

Everyone is here.

Booth 1. *A man, alone, a cup of iced water clasped in his hands. He wears 1982
like a costume: feathered hair, prodigious mustache, denim cutoff shorts, and
iron-on tank top, depicting dirt bikes in front of a dive bar. Carpenter boots and
a class ring. A living collector's item. Unopened, still in the cardboard-and-plastic
packaging, he'd be worth money. He is pale and haunted looking tonight, tense
and taut, as though he's unsure that this place is real, unsure that he's really
sitting here. Unease and desperate fear and relief trade places on his face. He*

furtively pushes his right hand—which for some reason is bright red—under the denim jacket that slumps beside him on the brown leather seat, lifts a corner, and looks under it. We can't see from here what he's hiding under there. His expression gives nothing away. He drinks his water dry and puts it at the edge of the table for a refill. He looks out the window at the dark trees, at the silent, leering moon. He checks under the jacket again. Panic is his companion tonight. It sits across from him, and he knows at any moment it might reach over the table and take him by the throat.

(earlier)

Bill Valerio sat astride the Toro mower like a red-shouldered king on a roaring, rolling throne. The hair on his freckled arms stirred in the breeze as he crested the small rise that marked the easternmost edge of the modest yard. Grass flew in slow motion up onto the twin movie screens of his mirrored sunglasses. Perspiration glistened, forming three thin streams along the finger-deep folds of his neck fat, gathering and rolling like a river down his back. His tongue poked out to taste the salty sweat in his mustache. With one hand, he turned the wheel left and aimed the whirring blades at a crescent of tall grass he'd missed on the first go-round. With the other, he adjusted the twisted shoulder strap of his tank top. His mind was fully immersed in the task, making order from disorder, drawing pleasing contoured lines in the frame around the prideful picture of his house.

It was a tick past high noon, the sun straight up in the blue sky, strewn with stretched-out, cotton-strand clouds. He had managed to make it through the hangover without puking up last night's burger and fries, to get his head above floor level, even to stand stooping in the shower as the cool water flattened his hair and coursed down between his shoulder blades. The night before, and into the morning, he'd spent kicking back on the umbrella-spangled deck of the King Crab with Kurt and Cal and Mikey, pounding down Natural Ice beers and rehashing all the old anecdotes, long since committed to memory, often recounted on boozy breath—the old standards. As indelible and seared-in as the classic rock from the Q-102, playing on the patio speakers, each opening chord met with a cheer signifying the thrill of the instantly recognizable. The waitresses were young and flirty, the food piled up and steaming hot, the mosquitos kept at bay by buzzing blue lanterns. The humidity was low, and the peanuts were plentiful. It wasn't quite high school, pounding Black Labels by the pond and staying up until the horizon went pink, but for middle age, it would have to suffice.

He'd even, he thought, finally forgiven Kurt for stealing Missy from him. At first, he'd wanted to kill the prick, kill them both: drive over to Kurt's to kill her in his bed and then on to the insurance company to drag Kurt screaming from his glass-walled office and hurl him three floors down into the courtyard to die among the plastic ferns, watching his blood pour out onto the diamond pattern of the ugly carpet.

But that was only fantasy. Over time, the humiliation had become a disagreeable yet somehow comforting companion. It was next to him when he woke up, sweating in his tangled sheets, it matched the speed of the Indian Roadmaster he rode five days a week to his shift at Leeds Electroplating, and it shone from the television, reducing his attention span to nothing and messing with his sleep on top of it all. Months of that. Now it was a ghost, fading in and out like a distant radio signal. It was almost gone. He was certain of it.

And last night, some old, syrupy Eagles song oozed from the speakers, and he'd looked over at Kurt, who was laughing a big fake laugh at something Mikey had said, a glob of mustard in his mustache. How could he be mad at Kurt after so long? He couldn't even remember what was so great about Missy. Sure, he missed the small, sweet things about living with her: her small footprints in baby powder on the bathroom floor, the two of them being the most stared-at couple in the King Crab or at 70s Night at Leeds Lanes, her light snoring that helped him finally fall away into sleep on sweltering summer nights.

But those were the old days, never to return. Whatever he had to offer, apparently it wasn't enough or wasn't right or . . . or something. She was pretty as the *Playboy* models that both troubled and sweetened his adolescence, but the reality of her was something to contend with. To hell with her. To hell with her daily crying jags and her endless bitching about the hags at her job. Let Kurt have her. Let him find out what she's really like.

Movement in his periphery shook him out of his brooding. Turning his head, he saw the source and slammed his foot on the brake, silenced the motor. It was a jogger, female, in tight shorts and a sweat-soaked green T-shirt, running along the curve of the cul-de-sac. But something was terribly, terribly wrong. Her neck was bent backward, folded, completely broken, though unbruised and unbloodied, and her head bounced around limply against her back, her upside-down, unblinking face staring blankly at the world behind her. She jogged back down the street, turned the corner, and was gone. He silenced the mower. Birdsong underscored by wind-ruffled leaves and the faraway barking of a dog . . . everything was as it had been. Everything but Bill.

With some effort and noise, he dismounted the mower and made a beeline for the front door. Cut grass gathered on his toes. The sun shone hot on his head. His heart trotted in his chest. The house bounced before him as he ran, real and solid and knowable. To his baffled relief, the doorknob did not break off in his hand, and the vestibule was as solid as you would want. Everything was whole, everything was real: the tiled floor, the framed picture of sunflowers, the nick on the wall made by the bureau from when he'd helped Missy move out on another dismaying day not so long ago. He grabbed the cordless phone from the kitchen table and on his third try successfully dialed 911. He tapped his foot impatiently as the ringtone sounded in his ear. He tried to gather his words.

"911. What is the location of your emergency?"

"There's a woman—an injured woman. She has a broken neck, um . . . badly broken."

"What is the location, sir?"

"Somerset Circle. I'm sorry. 25 Somerset Circle. S-O-M . . ."

"Is she breathing, sir?"

"She's, um . . . she's running, ma'am. She's probably on Long Farm Road by now."

"Running? With a broken neck?"

"Please send someone—just please send someone."

"They're on their way, sir."

He slid the phone into the pocket of his shorts and walked back to the foyer. The sweat had cooled, and its sour odor filled his nostrils. He was afraid to open the door, he found, afraid even to pull back the sidelight curtains and look outside. So instead, he stood, leaning slightly forward, and considered and immediately rejected a succession of rationalizations.

The knock at the door startled a grunt out of him, and he lurched forward and pulled it open. "I told the operator, she's not . . ." But the words fled.

Standing on the porch were two abominations that once had been police officers. Fat flies buzzed between and around them in clouds. The tallest officer floated about a foot off the porch. His neck was elongated, corrugated and collapsed, clouded with purple bruises. His eyes and tongue bulged, and he had swollen claws for hands. The second was a cadaver at the threshold of decomposition: sightless, cloudy eyes and slack lips, revealing the bottom row of teeth, all chipped and yellow. A too-white mannequin propped up oddly as though by invisible strings. The taller man attempted to speak, his dry lips trembling, emitting bubbling hisses and sputtering plosives. Tears of frustration formed in the red-brown swollen lids around his billiard-ball eyes. The two reeked of rot and shat pants.

"She went that way," Bill said, pointing down the road, scrunching up his face, trying not to breathe, just wanting these things away from him, far away. The floating officer turned and sailed back down the lawn to the car idling at the curve of the cul-de-sac. His partner leaned forward until his nose almost touched Bill's. Bill froze. The dead thing sniffed at him and shook his tattered head sadly. "The world is a tool," he said in a near whisper that seemed to come from somewhere other than his mouth, "and we don't know how to use it."

He turned and walked all herky-jerky down the lawn to join his partner in the car. The blue and red lights leapt into radiance and began to spin. The car sailed off down the street, turned the corner, and disappeared from view.

The fading reek still lingered in the house, so Bill fled to the outside and breathed in the air like a drowning man who'd found his way out of deep water. He felt a rush of heat, and the world around him tilted and brightened. Angling a hand at his brow, he looked up at the sun, squinting, now squeezing one eye shut. Pink-tinged bubbles formed on the surface of that great glowing ball, pushing themselves into strange shapes like oil in a hot pan. A thrumming sound, like a stadium full of cicadas, shook the ground as a red fissure formed and expanded within the sun, which then shimmied, shivered, and clove gently and silently into two halves. Each half went round, and the two new suns moved slightly apart and turned a strange orange-gray. They crumpled slightly, as though deflating. The sky coughed, and a thin, translucent, wrinkled film formed across its expanse, growing yellow and brown splotches like time-lapse mold.

Bill fell to his knees and leaned back, putting his hands over his eyes. Acrid saliva welled up over his tongue. He leaned forward and spat into the grass, his eyes squeezed shut and watering. He wiped at them with his hands, and when he opened them, he saw that the road had gone to water. Black water—not oil-black but deep wood-smoke black, reflecting no light. Topped with purplish foam, its countless pointed tongues lapped at the curb. And something new, something that for no reason he could name filled him with a stomach-clenching fear more than the splitting sun, more than the sky having succumbed to some kind of rot: chained to his mailbox, resting on his lawn, sat a wooden rowboat with a pair of oars in an X across the gunwale, a denim jacket draped over the seat.

Glass shattered at the neighbor's house, and the front door flew open. Out stumbled Warren Broadhurst, barefoot, clad only in boxers and a white T-shirt stretched taut over his prodigious belly. His throat lay open like a torn away door. Just inside the gaping hole, muscles moved like red ropes along scaffolding of bone. His face looked like some kind of badly done replica carved out of old wax. He clutched a large chef's knife and was cackling madly, stabbing at the air all around him. His eyes swung around and found Bill.

"Bill!" he shouted, his voice a painful-sounding rasp. "Everything's gone hinky."

As Bill watched speechless, Warren spotted the black water, and the knife slipped from his hand, its blade sinking into the earth. His voice slipped to a lustful whisper. "Look at it," he said. Rapture and awe filled his milk-white face. He lifted his T-shirt and threw it to the ground, yanked down and stepped out of his boxers.

"Warren, don't," Bill shouted. Or did he? He didn't know if he'd shouted, mumbled, whispered, or even just let the words roll around in his brain.

Warren was running toward the water now, the skin around his torn-out throat flapping, his little pecker bouncing, his belly high and round and pink. About four yards from the curb, he stopped, and his face reddened. Warren looked down. Bill followed his gaze. For a moment, it appeared that grass had sprouted from the tops of Warren's fat feet, but then Bill saw blood bubbling up and realized that grass had stabbed up through them.

All around Warren, the grass thickened and grew into long-nailed fingers. They tore at Warren's feet and calves, tearing furrows that filled with blood. He began to execute a high-stepping dance while shrieking. It was like some sort of demoniac burlesque show. At that thought, Bill burst into hysterical, uncontrollable laughter. Tears bubbled at his eyes and streamed down his cheeks. He was shaken out of it by a long, wavering shriek. Warren had come down funny on one ankle and crumpled into the grass, which grabbed at him from all sides and plunged into his body.

Through his sandals, Bill felt a slight tickle and then little stabbing pokes at the undersides of his feet. The fear expanded from his belly, plunging into his groin and shooting up into his chest, slithering up his spinal column and lighting up his beleaguered brain. He bolted for the rowboat like a cartoon man trying to run on hot coals. He leapt in, shifted the oars aside and fell onto the bench. He could not look at whatever was becoming of poor Warren. Hearing it was enough. He looked down the road to the cross-streets, where the black water churned and bubbled. He looked up at the strange new sky. His ears rang, and his tear ducts locked up. His heart slowed. And all at once, Bill Valerio put himself into a kind of existential Safe Mode, his non-essential components temporarily disabled. Most of the occipital lobe, sections of the temporal lobe—the parts of the brain that control reasoning and problem solving—went dark. His senses accepted input

> *the strange and shadowed sky*
>> *the black gelatinous water*
>>> *the withered man sinking into the many-fingered grass*

but no longer bothered with the hard work of interpretation. Arms dangling at his side, mouth slack and trembling, he slid the oars into their rowlocks, unhooked the chain that tethered him to what once had been real life, and pushed off into the unknown, the black waters slurping at the walls of the rowboat with lustful intent.

```
Abreçan Geist and the Hilltown
Ten : an oral history /
by Anne Gare, et al. -- 1st ed. --
Leeds : Gare Occult, c1961.
```

(from Chapter 2: Boyhood)

When you look at old pictures or film of a boy who is to one day become a great man, you search his eyes, his face, for the merest glimpse of that incipient greatness. By greatness, I do not necessarily mean goodness, virtue. Rather I refer to the ineffable quality that means a man will change the world in some substantial way. You think you see it in a narrowing of the eyes, a glint of atavistic intelligence maybe, or something knowing in the smile. But are you just reading in?

Here is Geist (at this point still Andrew Gass, his birth name before he reinvented himself in the wake of terrible events still a few merciful years away), sitting on a tree stump, cap on his head, squinting into the sun. He is clad in a white shirt with suspenders, short pants. Neat as a pin. Is there something in his smile?

Here he is with classmates. His posture is one of nascent authority, of an educator or a pontiff, perhaps a professor. Some of the other boys and girls stare at him with reverence, some with attentiveness. Some look at him with wariness as though watching a muttering man with an axe enter a café.

"Larger than life" is the term typically employed when speaking about the infamous and the notorious. It seems insufficient here. Here, the boundaries of life have been shredded and thrown to the farthest reaches. Geist is simply beyond, not a god so much as a filicidal father of gods.

A blinking light, red and yellow, found its way through Bill's eyelids, and a fluttering breeze danced through his lashes and over his face. He opened his eyes to the too-bright room, found Missy kneeling over him in a long T-shirt, flapping a Japanese paper fan at him. "Cut it," he muttered, and she tossed the fan back over her shoulder where it clattered into the basket of gels and shampoos and skin care products on her mirror-backed dresser.

She affected an exaggerated look of contrition and jabbed his collarbone with her index finger. "Get up."

He stretched out his arms and legs and arched his back and yawned mightily. He propped himself up on his elbows. The clock radio was blinking 12:00, 12:00, 12:00 . . .

"What the hell time is it?"

"Noon," she said. "And . . . noon. And noon and noon and noon. You never sleep this late. Musta needed it." She tilted her head at him. "Bill, get *up*."

"Let me just lie here," he said as she swung her legs off the edge of the bed and sat. He opened one eye to look at the sweetly familiar symmetry of her back as she yawned mightily, clasping her fingers and stretching her arms. As she stood and went to the mirror to brush her hair, he closed his eyes again and let the rhythmic rasp of the brush lull him into half-sleep. Soon though, a rising buzz moved about the room, and he opened his eyes to see a fly bumping against the ceiling.

"You wanna get that?" he said. Missy kept brushing her hair.

Another fly joined its cousin, and a third. Bill went to push himself up from the bed to grab something to swat them with and found that he couldn't move. He called again to Missy, but there was no sound, nothing but the tines of the brush against the skin of Missy's scalp, slowly subsumed by the rising buzz of a duet, a quartet, and then a symphony of flies, rising and falling, maddening. A fly landed on his nose, its legs tickling his skin. He could not reach up to wave it away. As he watched, cross-eyed, it crawled into his right nostril. Another landed on his upper lip and then more. One by one, they began to march into his nose. He felt them in there, little winged bundles of filth, pushing through, into his *head*, crawling around in the mysterious folds and ducts and hollows, enflaming his sinuses. They found their way down to his palate, and he opened his mouth to cry out, but instead, a stream of flies flew in to join their brethren. They filled his mouth like a restless crowd filing into a coliseum. He tried to blow them out, to spit them out, but to no avail. They crunched between his teeth, filling his mouth with rancid liquid. He couldn't gag. He couldn't breathe. He couldn't breathe . . .

Through his tears, through the fading blur, he could just make out Missy at the mirror, still brushing. Her hair was falling away in bloody clumps. She looked back at him, and her eyes were devoid of warmth, devoid of love.

He jolted awake. His back ached, and his stomach churned. He was stretched out on the floor of the rowboat, which was bucking and bouncing and creaking and cracking. Above him, that oddly stained and filmy sky trembled and flickered. Fighting nausea, he put his elbows behind him on the surface of the bench and pushed himself up to sitting. He expected to see something like rapids, churning foam, waves pumping up and down like the tips of drowned black tents. But the water all about him was calm and still, a black sheet lain over a flat surface. He saw no ripples, no wake trailing him, no evidence whatsoever of rough waters. The boat drifted gently parallel to the shoreline, just a few yards away. Bill stood tentatively to check the shore for houses to see if he could gauge how far the rowboat had taken him, but there were none, just steep, vine-veined riverbanks, climbing up to an impenetrable wall of entangled trees.

He looked over the edge of the boat and sniffed. The water, as far as he could tell, was odorless. Would it be safe to drink? His mouth was so dry. He touched the tip of his index finger to the surface. Cold. He felt a slight tingle. He lifted his finger, and a little white disk bobbed in the resulting ripple. Strange. Okay. No time like the present. He dipped his hand in the water. The tingling was fierce now, edging into pain. He lifted his hand and, for a moment, was baffled to see what appeared to be a white, almost translucent glove resting on the water's surface, and the realization hit him—it was a layer of skin. It crumpled and separated into a mass of strings. They bent and went rigid, and began to form some kind of strange pattern, bending and splitting off new branches. The structure rose up from the water like pin bones, forming something that looked like a tall, narrow tower. As the rowboat moved on, he watched uncomprehending as the structure climbed up into the sky.

Through the afternoon, he rowed through the endless Acheron. He fought sleep, fearing the idea of awakening again in a roiling estuary: before him the eternity of a great black sea, no shore in sight in any direction, an ocean that would kill him before long, wash away his flesh, build a strange, twiggy city from his skin, and bear his skeleton away into some baffling alien eternity. Also nipping at the edge of his thoughts was the terrifying prospect of approaching night, of the imminent revelation of whatever had become of—or worse, replaced—the moon and its twinkling adjutants.

Nothing to do about that though. Nothing to do but watch and wait.

And row.

He rowed and rowed until his arms hurt and sweat covered his body. At times, the riverbanks rose vertiginous and towering, higher than skyscrapers, at hard, right angles to the ground, the river a mere narrow ribbon not much wider than the boat itself, a stream between great towering cliffs, the diseased and peeling sky just a thin line impossibly high up. At one point, he could almost make out the tops of buildings: ramparts and parapets of stone, turrets like gapped teeth, spires like jousting lances, towers topped with pennants whose designs, if any, were obscured by shadow and distance. He saw no evidence of habitation, heard no voices, no trumpets nor drums. At other times the river broadened to the width of a five-lane freeway, and the banks sat low, nearly flush with the surface of the water. Feverfew and chicory vied for prominence at the water's edge, and unknown things slithered and chittered in the underbrush and the dense wood beyond.

Now it's nearing dusk. The sky is going a deeper brown, tinged with charcoal gray. Everything fades as that strange double sun falls below the tree line. There is no moon. No stars. No lights from the shoreline nor the cliffs, if there even are cliffs along this stretch of the river. No light at all. Even the colors he sees when he closes his eyes have fled. He can no longer feel the push of his backside against the bench, the clothes on his skin. He rubs his fingers together and feels nothing. He hears nothing but his own breathing . . . and even that begins to fade away into the silence. The last to go is his own inner voice—his only constant companion. It becomes a distant calling, too far to be able to make out the words. Then there are no words, just a faraway howl. Then nothing. The void. Annihilation.

Bill is gone.

And he's pulled back when a human voice shouts out from somewhere off to his right—a booming voice, unleashing a string of syllables that don't quite form into words. Bill flies back into his body, scrambles to his feet, shrieking. Both voices echo for a long time, but those echoes fade, and all returns to silence. Bill's heart beats wildly. He will not sleep again this night.

After a long time—*an hour?—two?*—a red glow appears up ahead, spanning a hazy black horizon. It brightens as he approaches. He closes his eyes tightly, and when he opens them, the boat is sliding along through a great, red-lit city. Above him at intervals of a quarter mile, great bridges arc, topped by spires and traversed by long, shining black trucks with multiple trailers. The shorelines are vast viaducts beyond which, to his left and his right, rise massive, many-windowed towers and the tall spikes of cathedrals, some topped with blinking blue lights. Some of the buildings curl over the river as though trying to get a look at him. He hears the thrumming of helicopters but does not see them. At one point, he hears cheers shot through with violence as from a packed stadium full of bloodthirsty cannibals cheering the presentation of freshly killed meat. At another, he hears a woman singing mournfully. Great shadows loom along the sides of stone walls and sink away. Bats dip and rise over the boat, chirping and trilling, some coming frighteningly close—so close Bill feels the disturbance of the air just over his head.

And then he is through, the city just a red glow somewhere behind him, and all is blackness again. Bill falls to sleep and wakes up to what now passes for daylight. The rowboat floats along a quiet stretch. Verdant fields like rumpled bedsheets roll away in all directions from each riverbank. The grass looks soft, lush, nearly as inviting as his own bed, the sheets freshly washed. Maybe Bill can guide the rowboat to the grassy shore, drag it onto land, and find someone who can make sense of what has happened to the world.

Fighting against some unnamable fear—that of breaking the status quo maybe—he does just that. He clambers from the rowboat and drags it up onto the grass and then goes to his hands and knees. The grass is cool, soothing, especially to his still-tingling right hand. He knows he should be wary that the blades might turn sharp, but he is all but overtaken with relief. The sky is still all wrong, the water too strange to countenance, that demonic city is still somewhere behind him, but he is off the goddamned boat and on land. He begins to walk. Ahead is a thin line of trees. He passes between two and enters a hilly meadow. A lone bird chirps, and the thin skin lining the sky ripples with a whisper.

Bill scans the horizon. There is movement in the distance. Cresting a far-off hillock, a squadron of shadows lurches and slides. They disappear and reappear over every hummock until they are finally revealed in the greenish half-light—they look like . . . they are . . . ventriloquist dummies. In seemingly inexhaustible numbers, they belly-crawl in Bill's direction, little elbows pushing into the ground, propelling them forward, glinting. Their loose, floppy, stitch-kneed legs trail behind them. Lightning flickers in dead eyes set over protruding cheekbones, and their mouths open and close in jerky unison as though they are all mouthing the same blasphemous prayer. They are clad in immaculate formalwear: tuxedo jackets and bow ties, tiny shoes shined, laces tied taut. In their tiny hands, they grip glimmering butcher knives.

Bill is, for just a moment, frozen. When he focuses on their over-large, hungry eyes, the spell is broken, and he beelines for the shore, looking behind him as he runs. He jiggers to the left and then the right, and they alter their course like magnetic filings. They're fast, the little buggers. With great reluctance, he clambers back into the rowboat and pushes away from the shore. They swarm into the water. The frontmost are just bobbing heads, wooden nostrils flared, brows arched, malevolence in their wooden eyes. The knives, which look sharp enough to slice through bone, are now clenched between white-lacquered wooden teeth. Bill rows furiously, but the water has thickened, and the boat lurches at a maddeningly slow pace. He looks ahead, and there is someone in the water. It's man, neck-deep, baldheaded, broad of shoulder. He grins and bobs like a fat buoy. "Allow one aboard," he says in a thin and frail voice that fades out and in like a radio station at the fringe of its range. "But only one." Then the man sinks slowly into the water, his eyes fixed on Bill until the water covers them. No ripples, no bubbles. Just gone.

A plastic hand curls up over the side of the rowboat. Bill grabs the dummy's floppy felt arm and pulls it forward. With his left hand, he pulls the knife from its mouth and flings it away. It catches one of the squadron of approaching dummies right in its forehead. That dummy's face goes green. Its eyes shoot out like billiard balls, landing in the water somewhere beyond the bow of the rowboat, and it rises to float on the water's surface, drifting off toward shore, the knife sticking up like a shark's fin.

Bill lifts his new boatmate up, under the arms, and places it on the other bench facing him. It lists to one side. Whatever had animated the thing has gone. The eyes stare sightlessly from their wooden sockets. The arms and legs lay limp. The other dummies angle away and head for shore, where they clamber up onto the grass and slither away.

Now Bill hears the distant and very welcome sound of traffic, of tires on pavement, squealing brakes, revving engines. The world around him ripples. The skin that holds the sky up flakes and falls away like singed confetti. Light floods Bill's vision, and he puts his arms over his eyes. The sounds grow louder. When he pulls his arms away, he's sitting cross-legged in a parking lot between two large SUV's. The light seems to indicate that evening is approaching. Alongside his leg rests his bunched-up denim jacket, a small rubber hand reaching out from beneath it. Bill stands on shaking legs and lifts the bundle to his side. Before him stands the Look Diner.

His stomach squeals, and hunger overtakes him. He crosses the lot and enters.

His eyes widen when he sees the glass jar of mints at the cashier's station. He grabs a handful and shoves them into his mouth. "Someone's hungry," laughs a frosted-blonde waitress. "You're going to need more nourishment than that." She snaps, and a thin teenage host appears, all bony shoulders and horn-rimmed glasses and acne-scarred cheeks.

"Table one," the waitress tells the host, and Bill follows him over. "Water," he whispers through a mouthful of mints. "Water."

The first has arrived.

Ring Bearer In Situ

THE LOOK DINER DRAWS INWARD SLIGHTLY, PULLING ITSELF CLOSE AGAINST the chill of evening. Restless gusts toss the treetops around and bounce the traffic lights on their lines. Emissaries of the wind sneak through the secret seams and concealed cracks of the building, causing the tablecloths to flutter, the tied-up coiffures of the waitresses to rustle and sway as they bustle their trays about. A quiet, high-pitched whistling underscores the piped-in hits of the eighties, nineties, and today. Above the dishwashing stations, steam hangs like horror-movie fog, enveloping the cooks and causing the grease on the grills to bubble and pop. The lights flicker. Here and there, they dim just slightly. Forks scrape plates, and diners and servers alike murmur excitedly.

Where is our grill man with the white hair and wiry arms? He's not at his station, not in the lobby nor the restroom. Scanning the lot, I see him now under the streetlight, letting the air cool the patina of grease and perspiration that lends his skin an unhealthy yellow glow. He looks like he's gathering all his strength, preparing it to be brought to bear. And he is regarding the scarred face of the gibbous moon, his head tilted as though he's listening intently. What is he preparing for? And what could the moon be telling him?

Charlene rolls the mop bucket onto the floor to clear a spill of pickle juice. The lights go low and lower until the restaurant is in a kind of dull brown twilight, and the mop is now a rope-thin, armless creature with pale, freckled skin and a face torn nearly in two by a shrieking mouth, bug eyes rolling wildly, its tangled hair soaked in blood. Charlene dunks the helpless, pale, naked thing's head into the bucket once, twice, a third time, and then slams it into the floor and drags it in widening circles, smearing blood in great streaky whorls. The smell, copper and iron and pickle juice, subsumes all other food-borne aromas. The piped-in music is jaunty and jocular. Charlene and the mop-man dance in the dim lights. It's a special night at the Look Diner, a propitious night. The kitchen staff, not knowing exactly why—maybe because the kitchen has achieved its optimum rhythm, maybe due to some inner, unacknowledged *connection*—pass around glances of merriment and camaraderie like champagne flutes.

Booth 2. A suit. That's the term for a man like him. An empty suit. The current occupant of this window-side booth, and of this particular suit—gray, tailored and pressed, pristine—is a slender, jaundiced man with an acne-cratered bald head and pink-rimmed eyes.

A suit.

The phrase is a shorthand designed to strip a man of his humanity. Call him a suit, call him an empty *suit, but what I see is a man in the throes of a struggle. He hasn't touched the two eggs whose pale yolks stare up at him with significantly less intelligence than that with which he stares back at them. Dave Strell is the name of the man in the suit, and he's rolling a certain idea back and forth between his thumb and forefinger, searching for the cancer.*

(earlier)

"State of the art climate control." That, verbatim, is how management described it eight months back when the staff stood in small clusters in a tree-bordered field as the middle managers posed in front of a mound of dirt with the just-for-show hard hats and the rusted-out shovels and the pained smiles. *Everybody smile. Rick, smile, buddy—it's a group picture, not a funeral. That's . . . better? Okay, let's take a few more. We'll use the best of five.*

State of the Art. Fresh air is drawn from the outside into the central system that, like a human nerve ending, detects its quality, its ambient temperature, its humidity. Compressors, condenser coils, and evaporators work in concert, pulling water from that air and pushing what remains through ducts that run like veins through the body of the building. The result is a responsive, even *hypersensitive* system, able to be fine-tuned by Building Services to make the air comfortable, dry and temperate whether the climate outdoors is that of a humidor or an igloo.

Climate. Dave Strell pulled a black kerchief from his desk drawer and daubed at the sweat that soaked the hair at the back of his neck. The trick, he'd found, was to remove oneself to a hallway or vacant conference room and to stand perfectly still, preferably directly under one of the vents. A clipboard in hand combined with a creased brow would provide the illusion of productivity by way of concentration and concern. His office, not so much an actual office as a shortcut between two hallways, was one of many avenues and nooks and corners that the "state-of-the-art climate control system" seemed to bypass, precincts where the vents breathed warmish air into warmish air in summer and in winter belched bursts of cold air like an asthmatic witch.

Control. In response to Dave's tempered pleas to management—one does *not* want to get tagged as a griper—Building Services had replaced a ceiling tile with a louvered vent and installed a grate in the bottom half of each door. The net effect: nil, naught, nothing. Dave rose and stretched, daubed again at his neck, and exited the office, clipboard in hand, off to his second break of the day. He shot a defiant look at the hall camera as he passed. The lens blinked in reply.

```
Abrecan Geist and the Hilltown
Ten : an oral history /
by Anne Gare, et al. -- 1st ed. --
Leeds : Gare Occult, c1961.
```

(from Chapter 2: Childhood Cut Short)

Augustus Gass was regarded by his workers and his acquaintances as a taciturn bull of a man, short of temper and singularly unwilling to brook nonsense. He presented from behind his great oak desk a gruff visage, mouth pulled down into a perpetual grimace, baleful eyes peering from under a wild-thatch brow, like a malevolent creature stalking its prey from under a partially uprooted tree. He eschewed idle talk and spared no one the fury of his tongue when he deemed it warranted. There was a wager among his men as to whether the man could affect a smile that was not pained. Even at Sunday worship, it was a grave, joyless face he raised to regard his creator.

At home, however, Augustus was a man his employees would scarcely have recognized: a doting and loving father to his only son. He was forty-two at the time of Andrew's birth, and despite the face he presented to the outside world, he was unrestrained in his joy. He delighted in every burp, every vocalization, in the merest gesture from his boy. He would lift the infant heavenward, cradled in his rough-hewn hands, and scrunch up his face, causing Andrew to squeal and giggle. He would throw the boy onto his shoulder and roam from room to room, narrating the history of each piece of furniture, the stories behind the art on the walls, the biographies—sometimes made up from whole cloth—of the neighbors who passed by on the street or tended to their lawns or sat rocking on their porches in the glinting sun.

Andrew's mother Victoria was of diminutive stature, thin as one of Augustus's arms, wispy haired and pale to the edge of translucence. She dressed neatly and modestly and often bore a shy and secretive smile. One had to lean forward to hear her voice, and in doing so, one was typically rewarded with a sharp-tongued remark or a sly witticism. Like her husband, she showed a remarkably different character at home—warm and wise but fuller in voice and freer in movement and gesture. And she could match, if not best, Augustus when it came to verbal vulgarities. Their close acquaintances and servants tell of how the two often laughed wickedly together and then vowed—through snorts and snuffles but with all seriousness—to confess their sins the very next Sunday at mass.

The couple's happiness was never in question. They doted upon one another and on Andrew. Their infrequent rows were quiet and, though not free of tension, evinced a mutual deference, and they refrained from sequestering themselves. So they supposed, the boy might learn to navigate his way through the potentially treacherous straits of disagreement when he was old enough for courting.

It was a gray November morning when Andrew saw his father emerge from the bedroom, pale and unsteady on his feet. The boy saw something that day in his father's face that he had never before seen: worry. Augustus hastened to the office of Doctor Marsh, foregoing work, another startling event without precedent. The next time—and last—Andrew saw his father, he lay in a hospital bed in a haze of morphine and the mephitic odors of mortality.

Stunned and bereft, Victoria sailed like a ghost through Andrew's life. She fed him, sat silently with him in the darkened living room, spoke only when necessary, and held her face in her hands. One black morning, he woke to the sounds of clamor and many voices, and he walked half-asleep to the brightly lit kitchen where he found a milling, mumbling crowd of uncles and aunts and strangers, some of whom he recognized from having seen them at his father's funeral. He rubbed his eyes, searching the group for his mother, and was then spied by Aunt Wilhelmina who ran to him, lifted him to her breast, and held him tightly. From that vantage, he saw the body on the floor, cloaked in white blankets. She looked impossibly small, as though death had taken something of her person as a trophy. That day, he had awakened in his home, but that night he fell to troubled sleep in an unfamiliar and shadow-furnished place—the rambling estate of his aunt and uncle, who he barely knew, though he was aware that his mother and father shunned Uncle Samuel, Augustus's brother, owing to an irreconcilable difference in their faiths.

Dave had known the very moment the invitation appeared in his inbox. When your supervisor calls a meeting with just you and human resources after weeks of difficulties and unaccounted for alterations in your duties, there are no alternate interpretations, no other possibilities. It made sense in a flash, all of it: them giving him work that previously had been the province of ten others—a move that at the time had seemed to Dave not sinister but merely backward. Add to that the assigning of menial tasks, the piling on of duties with—he saw it now!—the underhanded motive of overwhelming him, weakening him, forcing flaws and encouraging errors. Praise ceased. Ideas he brought up were dismissed with contemptuous dismissiveness or else simply passed over without comment.

And he had ignored all of this at his peril.

The meeting was scheduled for one o'clock. The email had been sent three hours earlier, an act of cruelty in itself. After scanning the email, which contained only the invitation with neither corresponding text nor agenda, and responding with a click of the mouse, Dave grabbed his day planner and fled to the cafeteria. Just a few workers were seated there: people he didn't know, young people, mostly grouped by the windows, staring into their phones or picking at blueberry muffins or browned scrambled eggs. Dave sat at a table in the far corner under a painting of a wheat field under a cloud-filled sky, opened his day planner to a blank page, and began drawing concentric circles. At twelve thirty, he stood up on wobbly legs and made his way to one of the private restrooms. He put the day planner on the corner of the sink, and until ten minutes to one, he stood with his hand on the wall, staring down at the commode, intermittently dry heaving. Then he went and sat at his desk to stare at the blank computer screen.

Three minutes before the meeting, Dave's supervisor, Bill Papirio, materialized at the open wall of Dave's cubicle, all knit eyebrows and gelled hair in unruly spikes. Papirio had been promoted to manager three months back, another in a parade of unwitting beneficiaries of the company's unspoken policy of promoting people arbitrarily, putting them in charge of former colleagues, and proceeding to provide them with no training and no guidance. Dave suspected that in Papirio's case, it was something to do with the affectations of calmness and rationality that masked a smoldering smorgasbord of insecurities.

Papirio was holding his own day planner tightly at his side, as though stanching an open wound. Dave rose, and Papirio, saying nothing, turned and with a brief and almost snide wave of the hand beckoned Dave to follow. Here then was a further indignity: being walked like a dog to one's disciplinary meeting.

The route to the human-resources office was a long one: down the main hall of the building, past the administrative offices, the laboratory, the loading dock. Dave walked behind his superior, staring sharp needles at the pink splotches on the back of Papirio's neck. They walked in silence—and in semi-darkness as most of the hall lights were off, bulbs unscrewed, another in a ceaseless parade of petty cost-saving measures. (The month before, the kitchen drawers that once held coffee were emptied, leaving grounds like dirt scattered on a casket lid.)

Carol, the HR director, greeted them warmly, as though the too-bright office were her home, as if they were equals about to have a casual conversation. The three sat, and Papirio opened his planner and pulled out a pocket folder full of forms. "Dave," he said, his voice flat as he began to recite the words he'd clearly rehearsed all morning, "I have noted on several occasions deficiencies in your performance, and I'm afraid that despite my best efforts to redirect you, I've just not seen the improvement we had hoped to . . . so what we're going to do is implement what we call a performance improvement plan. This is a *positive* thing, David. Our focus, the three of us, will be on your performance. Not you working for yourself but a team focused with an almost . . . *atomic* intensity upon you. But be warned: ultimately, your fate is on your neck. Should we see even one slip, one violation of the tenets of the plan I am about to hand you, there will be no chance for redemption, no options left. Your termination will be immediate and permanent."

Kim sat splayed on the bench in the glass-walled smoking shelter that mimicked a bus stop, keeping company with a beige, ash-stained smoking receptacle. The shelter sat forty yards or so from the front doors of the main building, looked over by rows of tinted-glass windows like sunglass-shielded eyes. Dave loosened his tie and sat a respectful distance from her. With both hands, he scratched at his hairline and then stretched, his shirt coming untucked in the process. In the woods that bracketed the corporate campus—two buildings connected by a pedestrian bridge—cicadas moaned in rounds, and the birdsong was subdued as though somewhere a giant battery was running out. The sun was a bright smear. "It's cooler," he said. "Out here."

"The condemned man speaks," Kim said. She hugged herself and affected a shiver. "It's freezing, Dave. Fetch me a hot toddy."

Her voice lowered in imitation of a television reporter. "So Dave," she said, holding out an invisible microphone, "tell my audience how it feels to be on the dreaded performance improvement plan."

"All that means," Dave said, "is that the relationship is over, the magic is gone, and it's a race to get out before they throw you out."

"But how does it *feel*?"

"Like walking on the surface of a bubble."

"And how do *you* feel?"

"Stronger than dirt."

Kim seemed to find the answer satisfactory. The two sat for a time in silence, lost in their own reveries. It was a little after quarter to four in the afternoon— they had discussed often enough the interminable stretch, that slowing of time itself, that occurred mid-afternoon until four, a time that signified the approach of the end of the working day, a time to let a certain slackness creep in, to start considering dinner and the subsequent, merciful shutting down of consciousness—if luck allowed—for the night. They were so close.

Sensing movement in his periphery, Dave turned to see Manny Firth approaching at a shambling jog, his belly jiggling, his tie askew. *Someone's shooting up the building,* Dave thought, and it amused him that it was a positive one.

"Meeting!" Manny shouted, his voice high and hoarse. "All-company meeting!"

Kim groaned, let the groan slide into a growl. "A meeting," she said. "At four o'clock. On a Friday."

The gathered employees turned and shifted and chattered in their chairs. Dave sat next to Kim in the last row. A door at the back of the room opened an inch and then another and then just enough to let slide through the CEO. He was tall and splay-fingered with a crooked nose and a thin mouth that seemed situated too far down on his face. It was a rare thing to see him in the halls, and when he was spotted, he moved quickly, keeping close to the wall, visibly flinching and twitching as others passed him in the opposite direction.

Not much was known about him. The name plate on his door read Dr. 999, and those who spoke with him addressed him as simply Doctor. He spoke infrequently, in low tones, and with many hesitations and long pauses and alarmingly violent throat-clearings.

Standing now at the microphone, he executed one of those throat-clearings. Bravely, he did not turn his head nor shield his mouth with his hand. Feedback harmonized with him. The assembled crowd grimaced and scowled as one, some theatrically raising their hands to their ears. Their chatter ceased.

After a pause, he spoke into the silence. "When a company has conquered all it can on earth, what is next? Why envision an impenetrable ceiling and not simply a cloud that mimics a solid mass, a mist that can be punched through as easily as a plane of air, a stratum of wind? Today, we are going to launch a hostile takeover. On the afterlife."

He grinned, his nostrils flattening, his eyes narrowing to gleaming slices. The interior of his mouth seemed to consist mainly of reddened gums with just the edges of teeth pushing through.

"All communications from inside this building," he continued, "have been cut off."

Dave dug out his phone and was greeted with a blank screen. All around him, his coworkers fumbled their phones from their pockets, fished them from their purses, to find the same. A rumble shook the room as a steel curtain rolled down outside the windows behind the CEO, cutting out the daylight, causing the floor to tremble slightly. The lights in the room brightened.

"We will need one of you to stay behind to fulfill a final function here on behalf of the company. How though to determine just who? After many hours of deliberations spread out over a period of months, the board has agreed upon a contest." A glowing screen descended from the ceiling. The crowd's eyes rose to regard a photograph: overexposed, in a corona of light, a pile of rings, ornate of design and clearly ancient, scattered across a conference table.

"Retrieve these items," said Dr. 999. "They have a significance that must for now, to you, remain a mystery. A careful examination of the diaries and notes of the company's founder tells us that the right person will find them and will be guided thereafter by an unseen hand. The rest of us will storm the ineffable while you, the person who locates and retrieves these artifacts, will perform the vital concluding ceremonies of the old company here on earth.

"The outer doors are locked and sealed. The windows are blocked. There is no egress. Soon I will release you from this room, and your search will begin. For your convenience and comfort and in the interest of keeping your energy high, the cafeteria shall remain open."

His eyes fluttered and rolled up, showing only red-veined white. He raised his hands, palms up. A sheen of sweat stood out on his cheeks and lips. His eyes shifted from side to side. His face stiffened, and his voice went higher as he started in on a lilting, wavering chant.

All my life
(all his life)
I have studied
(he has studied)
the patterns of birds

(the patinas of bards).
Their movements before storms
as though they were smeared stains of ink
(bleared brains at the brink)
on an undulating blanket of steely gray sky
(freely say I).
Dog's water and barrel pigs
(frog slaughter, imperiled figs)
mark thine hand and pock my eye with grit.
Hove by space,
hewn by light,
pushed through flesh in search of stone.
(touched to cleft, a church of bones).

"In the preceding," Dr. 999 said, "I have provided a clue as to the location of the items. In a moment, you may go forth. When the items are found, we will . . . collect the rest of you. Then our journey will commence.

"One last thing. I am as of now dissolving management. You are hereby free from the inequities of the corporate structure, arbitrary hierarchies, falsehoods designed to squelch and stifle. You answer to no one and are beholden to no one. If you came to me today in shackles, those shackles have crumbled to powder.

"The laws that govern outside these walls have no voice and no agency here.

"Go now."

The doors at the back of the meeting room swung open.

Abrecan Geist and the Hilltown
Ten : an oral history /
by Anne Gare, et al. -- 1st ed. --
Leeds : Gare Occult, c1961.

(from Chapter 2: Childhood Cut Short)

Andrew Gass was pulled from his fog of loss into the bright, blinding light of terror at a vaudeville show held with great fanfare on the stage at the Leeds Academy of Music. In his diaries, he recalls the scene. Seated between his laughing, clapping aunt and uncle, he sat numbly before the spot-lit spectacle of prancing, capering minstrels, fearsome tigers with bared fangs, sharp-tongued blondes in garters and top hats, grinning clowns, and magicians in flowing capes. After a dark, death-riddled act by a magician named Spettrini, the stage and the entire hall went dark. The crowd's murmur hushed to a whisper. Then a single spotlight shone upon a nondescript man seated on a stool, a doll supine in his lap. When the doll raised its wooden head and began to speak, young Andrew's eyes went circular, and his breath caught in his throat. The doll exuded menace: the thick, knife-sharp eyebrows rising and falling over too-huge eyes, the straight white teeth, the fat little clenched fists and dangling legs. Andrew watched it as one watches a strange dog at the edge of a playground.

That night—and many nights after—Gass was subjected to terrible night-spanning dreams, featuring the ventriloquist dummy. It sat in tree limbs before smoky sunsets. It rose slowly from the murky water between his feet in the bath, its eyes covered in suds, water spilling from its terrible open mouth. Its felt arms extended, winding like ribbons around Andrew's arms, trapping him, pulling his face close to its own horrible visage, and nipping at his lips with sharp, lacquered teeth. It beckoned from behind the iron gates of ancient boneyards. It spun filth-strewn webs in high corners like a grinning spider.

Rather than face those dreams, he fled to the towering bookshelves of his uncle's study. Grantham, Augustus's brother, was rumored to have trafficked in the black arts, though many who knew him had scoffed: he was merely a collector of occult books and ephemera and trinkets, they'd said. Andrew was allowed free reign in the library, and it was there the lonely boy spent much of his time, emerging for meals only reluctantly as it was at meals that he had to face the pitying eyes of Grantham and Wilhelmina. Even as he ate, he found himself longing to get back to the books.

Dave Strell wandered the gray halls in a daze. A smell like burning plastic and fibers filled the air, and clouds of smoke prowled the halls like conjoined clusters of ghosts. Through the smoke before him came a two-armed, ten-legged, kicking thing as wide as the hall itself, resolving finally into a group of coworkers, arms entwined behind one another's necks, kicking and clomping. They laughed, baring their teeth at Dave, as he moved to the side, pressing his back against the wall to let them pass. Somewhere in the distance, someone cackled, and then a thud sounded, and a pleading voice. Another thud and the voice was silenced.

Just outside a photocopier alcove, Paul from the Finance Department sat inside a perfect circle of black, among the plastic shards of a pried apart toner cartridge. With blackened fingertips, he smeared the powder across his cheeks and forehead and pushed around what remained of his hair. He spotted Dave, and his eyes widened, lending him an unfortunate aspect. He hissed, teeth a bright, shining blue.

Dave gave Paul a wide berth and continued down the hall. He turned a corner and glanced upward just in time to see a ceiling tile bulge and split, spilling Steve from File Management to the floor in a snowy squall of perlite and asbestos. Steve was a diminutive man, pin neat and perpetually in a fret, interrupted occasionally with moments of high pique. Dave heard the man's neck crack when he hit, saw his fingers twitch and grab at the air. He knelt and turned Steve over onto his back. He smoothed the man's gray hair, used his middle and index fingers to shut his eyelids. As he stood to wander on, slightly stooped, Steve's eyes snapped open, unseeing.

In the path between two warrens of cubicles, Grey from Facilities and a couple of young interns in sweater vests had spread out blueprints and architects' sketches of the building. They were conferring, consulting, jotting down notes, and sticking red push pins into the documents. As Dave approached, they quieted and stared at him warily. He shrugged and moved away, and they resumed their chatter.

From the far corner, "Randy" Jerry emerged from between two potted, plastic ferns in a tangle of manufactured straw. He was in his mid-sixties, eternally harried, and for the past few months had begun to talk incessantly (and insufferably) about his impending retirement. He'd earned his nickname by way of a brave co-worker, since fired, who sneaked into Jerry's cubicle and discovered that he'd been working while listening to a pornographic audiobook. Jerry's shirt lay untucked. Beads of dried blood formed a crescent across his forehead. His chewed nails worried at the fat of his belly. He grabbed from atop a file cabinet a guillotine-style paper trimmer and threw it to the floor. With one foot, he stepped on the platform, and he wrenched the bladed arm from its socket, splintering the wood and sending screws flying across the carpet.

Jerry spotted Dave and smiled broadly—the smile not quite reaching his eyes.

He approached, swinging the blade in wide arcs. His comb-over came unstuck from the top of his head and flopped about, a loose shade in a windstorm. His lips moved oddly, and when he got into hearing range, Dave realized the man was chirping and chirruping like a cat who's spotted a plump little sparrow. Dave took a few steps back and unhooked the fire extinguisher from the wall. He lifted it with two hands and waited for Jerry to get within striking distance.

```
Abrecan Geist and the Hilltown
Ten : an oral history /
by Anne Gare, et al. -- 1st ed. --
Leeds : Gare Occult, c1961.
```

(from Chapter 3: Casting off the Shell)

Meredith Corbett (Former Classmate). After Andrew's parents died, he kind of came out of his shell. I don't think I'd heard him say more than a few words at a time before then, and even those under his breath. We all flocked to him. Maybe because he blasphemed in ways that no one else would have dared. He was *funny* . . . I mean, he was angry. It was sometimes scary how red his face got and how he cursed . . . but he called God a fat-arsed kidnaper, the apostles a passel of sycophantic, white-robed masturbators. He savagely parodied epistles and sang bawdy satires of the songs from our hymnals. The teachers caught wind of this, but it was almost as though they were afraid of Andrew. They *tut-tutted* and turned a deaf ear.

One day in the early morning, he'd gotten himself into the locked school somehow and into Mrs. Guiley's mathematics classroom. He filled the chalkboard top to bottom and side to side with numbers and symbols. I recognized some of the symbols from the textbooks, but the others I'm pretty sure he made up. They bothered me. Can't tell you why. Like the way you feel when you look at something you're not supposed to. A dirty picture or a murder book. Mrs. Foxglove erased the board, but you could still see the symbols, taunting-like, ghosts that stared at you from behind whatever she wrote on the board that day. And when she erased her day's work, Andrew's symbols would get clearer again. Three days later, Principal Meyer walked in to inspect the board. He was a priest as a young man but gave up the priesthood to become a math teacher, like advanced math, and he ended up the principal. Anyway, Meyer saw what was written on the board, and all the veins jumped out on his face and neck and on his wrists. He fell to his knees so hard that the wood floor cracked, and then he just dropped dead right there on the spot. You can still see the split wood.

Well, Andrew snickered. The other kids started in too, laughing and slapping their knees. Mrs. Foxglove was trying to revive the principal and scold us at the same time. But I saw something nobody else did. I've never spoken of it to anyone to this day.

Mrs. Foxglove herself raised a gloved hand to her mouth to cover her own laughter.

"The D-35S has a self-sharpening system," said Jerry.

He was sitting on the floor like a kindergartener, his plump legs in a Y. The bladed arm lay a few feet away on the carpet like a severed limb. Blood cascaded in curtains from Jerry's upper forehead, masking his face in dark red. He spat and sputtered, sending droplets skyward. His pants had split, revealing a patch of threadbare cotton underpants. *Tighty-whiteys*, thought Dave, and he stifled a laugh for fear that if he started he might not be able to stop. "Give up, Jerry," he said.

Dave had stove in Jerry's head with the heel of the extinguisher, which now lay like roadkill by the wall, foam dripping from its metal jaw. Dave stepped closer, saw the edges of the remaining skull through the torn-away flesh. Beyond that ragged window, the surface of the brain bobbed in blood and yellow fat. Jerry looked up at him with one dilated eye, and the other, bulging from its socket, stared off at an odd angle as though sizing up the power outlet on the hallway wall.

"I bought them with my own money," he said. "Shabber. Shab. Shabb-wer. *Show*-er curtains. Because of mildew."

Dave considered grabbing the extinguisher and finishing the job—a final act of mercy. But somehow, he hadn't the stomach for it. Yet he couldn't watch either.

He heard Kim's voice coming from one of the employee kitchens. He left Jerry mumbling and bleeding and headed her way. Through the glass, he saw that the door of the refrigerator lay in the middle of the kitchen among disassembled sandwiches and yogurt cups oozing sugared fruit. Kim stood at the open fridge, blocking Dave's view. He stepped on a yogurt cup to get her attention, and she whipped around, a letter opener in each hand. She smiled. Behind her, Bill Papirio was wedged into the refrigerator. He was whining, the high-pitched squeal of a frightened dog. Blood splotches stood out on his light-blue shirt.

"You know what this all means, Dave," Kim said. "This is the Solar Temple. This is Jonestown. It's—who were the people with the sneakers and the track suits? Heaven's Gate. This is *company-sponsored mass suicide*. Sure will save them a lot of money in severance pay." She turned back to address Papirio. "I didn't participate in the Walk for Health, and I'm sure as hell not participating in this." She lunged forward, drew a bright-red line down Papirio's cheek with the letter opener. The man screamed.

"Let me see that," Dave said. She handed him the letter opener. He approached the man wedged into the refrigerator. He felt his ears going red, rage surging up into his brain.

"Bill," he said, "*your* termination will be immediate and permanent."

When it was done, Kim was gone. There was no one in sight. The halls were obscured in a haze—figures moved back in there somewhere, maybe, or maybe they were just in his imagination. The tangled mess in the refrigerator he couldn't seem to make himself look at. He didn't know what it was, but he knew he wanted no part of it. In his head, Dr. 999's words ran over and over again, reformed into new phrases. The patterns of birds. Dog's water. Pig bladder. In search of a church of bone. Eye with light. Hewn with grit. Patinas. Steely ink. Faces of frogs. Convenience and sky. Comfort and stone. The cafeteria shall remain open.

The location of the items . . .

It came to him with an almost physical thud of revelation. And then the gunfire started.

(excerpt from the childhood notebooks of Andrew Gass)

Someone, some cousin or another with a fat rat-face and greasy hair and buckteeth, told me Mum and Dad were in a better place now and that god must of

*(sic) needed them in heavan (sic). I didn't answer him. I couldn't even look at him.
I need them more than stupid god does. It's not fair that they are just gone gone
gone. And they will be gone when I am twelve and when I am sixteen and when
I am thirty-two. And I sat with them in those wooden pews and stood up and sat
down at the whim of that chinless possum of a priest and said the words along
with everyone, and I looked around at them sometimes when we were supposed
to have our eyes squeezed shut in the holy joy of god's love or some such lie, and
they looked such fools that I had to laugh. A flock, they call themselves, and a
flock is right—a flock of drooling sheep with no light in their eyes and no spark.
And it was all storys (sic) and lies and everyone trying to please a god who would
not be pleased, who begged for praise like a dog begs for scraps at the table, who
demanded that no one cast an eye on another god, like a husband with a legion
of wives who demands faithfulness from each and all. A thief and a tyrant and
a brat. A mewling, spoilt god. And he said don't bow to graven images, and they
read those words in a room full of leering, pain-faced wooden christs and robed
men shaped in colored glass. And crucifixes, hundreds of them, in wood and
stone and steel and bone. I have come to hate the sight of a crucifix, such a simple
symbol for simple people. I want to sharpen their ends and turn them to knives,
make them useful. And I have come to hate the sight of a church with its solemn
grounds and its squared-off hedges and its taunting steeples and its earnest face
behind which they speak of blood and broken seals and covenants and half-naked
men nailed to wood. And they dare speak my parents' names in their filthy prayers.
I want to pull the words from their tongues with an animal's claws and light them
on fire on the walk and smear my face with their ashes. There is so much I want
to do. There are not enough lifetimes to dismantle every church and stomp their
bricks to powder and hang their priests from the telephone poles of every city
where a man died and the priest spoke barely of the man and instead told lies of
the Imposter Jesus and his sermons of lies and mockery. I do not want my name
in their mouths. I denounce my Christian name and my family name. I am not
the child who sat in the pew and mouthed nonsense, smug in the certainty that I
would never be alone and that Mum and Dad would always be there to protect me
and guide me. I am something different now. I am sin and blasphemy, and I shine
with something the opposite of light. And I need to make my mark on the world.*

The gunfire sounded like a stuttering heart: tachycardia, the rapid thumping of blood forcing its way through overtaxed arteries. It seemed to come from all directions but relatively far off, at least for now. Still, it rattled his ribcage, upset his stomach, sent his thoughts scattering, spiraling like smoke trails away from coherence. What did it mean? Were Dr. 999 and the board killing the staff? Why now? Had someone already found the rings? As Dave approached the long, shadow-strewn corridor at whose end the cafeteria lay, everything seemed to fade into the far distance.

A thought had begun to pick at the edges of his mind. He would have sworn that the office campus did not have a cafeteria. Twelve years ago, he'd spent several months between jobs, temping at an insurance company. *That* office had a cafeteria—a salad bar, a sandwich station, a couple of grills, a coffee area, and a row of toasters. But if this place had one, he'd have known, wouldn't he? He tried to picture it, but his mind could conjure up only the insurance company cafeteria and the cafeterias at various hospitals. No, there was no cafeteria here. People ran out for takeout, met food delivery drivers in the lobby, or brought in sandwiches in brown-paper bags. He couldn't remember anyone carrying one of those Styrofoam clamshell boxes. Not here.

Maybe he was just exhausted. Certainly, there was a cafeteria. Hadn't Dr. 999 said as much? Hadn't he himself gone there to await his disciplinary meeting?

And there it was, just ahead, its entrance flanked by signs advertising turkey burgers and promoting the eating of greens. Dave pushed the doors open and entered.

The cafeteria was a scene of carnage. Bodies piled on the salad bar, strewn with julienned carrots, green peppers browning at the edges, the scattered yellow crumbs of coagulated egg yolks. There was Mary, the elderly receptionist, flowered dress yanked up to reveal a grayed and frayed girdle, face down in a tray of beets. Frank from IT draped face-up over the sneeze guard with his shirt torn, zipper down, massive belly exposed like a sun-bleached cliff, lips torn and bleeding, mouth stretched open, stuffed to bursting with a glut of red onions, lashes flattened and face soaked in tears, dried mucous clotted under his nose.

A cook, tall and heavy, in thick glasses and the beginnings of a goatee, stood at the grill in a fog of steam: his chef's whites and apron torn, revealing a nest of black hair, each hand gripping a chef's knife, both knives dripping with blood. Dave recognized him as the cook from the insurance company, behind that grill every day, overcooking burgers, scattering onions, scraping the gunk to the back, barely able to conceal his exasperation with entitled managers who cajoled and demanded and ridiculed and treated him like something less than human.

The cook seemed to undulate in the air, his sides expanding and contracting, the skin on his hairy arms restless, twisting and circling the muscle. His hair went white, and his arms thinned. His goatee sunk back into his skin. His torso shrunk as though vacuumed from within. His face creased with age and pockmarks, and his cheeks sunk to rest against his teeth and hug his chin tightly. His eyes narrowed. The skin came to rest. Everything went silent, save the drip, drip, drip of blood hitting tile. That face rang far-off, distorted bells deep in the folds of Dave's brain—from where did he know it?—and something cold and bristly slithered along his spine and made goose pimples stand up all over his body like logorrheic braille. A flash of lightning and all was back to whatever "normal" had become.

The chef locked eyes with Dave. "No one will get them," he said. "They tried. They were animals. But it wasn't enough." The chef looked heavenward, his neck stretching slightly, his lips pulling tight over his teeth. Dave followed his gaze, saw nothing, and looked down. Strange shapes stood out under the skin of the cook's straining neck, between the veins and the platysmal bands that stood out like the roots of ancient trees—the rings. They appeared to be shallowly placed, not terribly deep into the flesh. Dave could almost make out the silver tinge through the man's pale skin. He looked around him for a knife, saw none. He bared his teeth, crouched, and leapt. His teeth were fangs, his nails claws. He tore open the flesh of the surprised cook's neck with his teeth, plunged his nails into the man's ears and eyes.

Afterward, he stood in the washroom. Splashing his face, he regarded himself in the large mirror over the sinks. His suit was free of blood. He looked good. Younger. No more acne scars. He stretched open his lips to reveal immaculate white teeth. No fangs, he noticed, and his hands were just normal human hands, his nails trim and neat, unchewed, cuticles intact. He cupped one of them just below his lower lip and spat the rings into his palm. He pocketed them and exited into the lobby of the Look Diner. Well, what the hell. The cafeteria was tainted, he was hungry, and he needed to get the taste of blood out of his mouth.

Goat's Rue

THE DINERS STAB THEIR FORKS INTO THEIR PLATES, AND THE CEILING fans whip around, trembling and shaking, lending a strobe effect to the lighting. The whole restaurant wobbles like a misaligned carousel tray in a microwave. I feel it too, the visual illusion provoking in me a deeply unpleasant physical response that is concentrated around my midsection and my head. And you're looking a little green yourself. I'll order you up a ginger ale. One for me too. Settle our stomachs.

It smells like something burning, doesn't it? Look—black smoke curls in a long, looping tendril from the kitchen, a tentacle of deep black, searching the restaurant . . . it hits Marti's ankle as she stands, talking to Charlene, sneaking glances at the white-haired grill man, snapping the gum in her mouth. The tendril rolls up her leg and slides up into her skirt. She grimaces, reaches back, tugs at her underwear. The tendril retreats as though chastened, begins to wriggle along the floor this way and that, its tip rising and falling as though it's sniffing at the air.

The ceiling tiles begin to flake. The flakes fall like snow. The white-bearded man at the center table grabs the shoulders of his female companions and pulls them in close to him. He raises his tongue and catches the flakes on his swelling tongue. His eyes are wide open and wild. The ladies do the same. They morph into a three-headed dog, an abomination. Their red-and-purple tongues flicker like flames.

Booth 3. *A white-haired woman whose furrowed hand trembles piteously as she raises her teacup to her pale lips. She is otherwise as still as a stone in roaring, frothing rapids. She wears a flowered blouse. Next to her in the seat sits a crumpled duffel bag. She's unaffected by the trick of the lights and the ceiling fans. While the other diners grip the arms of their chairs or each other's shoulders for support, she rests her arms lightly on the table. She is unable to hide her emotions from her face. They are as clear as the billboards that line the nearby highway. She is anxious now, irritated by the noise of her fellow diners. Relief flutters across her features. It morphs into indecision or a restlessness, the strong urge to do something specific yet tinged with frustration at not knowing exactly what that thing is. She steeps the teabag needlessly, pushes it down with her spoon, and takes another trembling sip.*

Earlier. How quickly it had all gone wrong. Jeannine had stepped off the path to relieve herself, calling out her intention to Missy and Miles, who had some time back stopped any pretense of moderating their pace so she could keep up. She could just make out their matching backpacks bouncing along, far up ahead, just at the point where the path took a sharp southward turn. She couldn't tell whether they'd heard her. Oh well. They'd have to come back for her when they realized she wasn't behind them anymore. Maybe then they'd see how self-involved they were.

She circumnavigated a deadfall that looked like a jumble of thorny crowns piled against the sheared-off stump of what once must have been a massive, old oak. She walked carefully, arms out like a tightrope walker, down a mild incline to a shady, leaf-domed grotto and squatted by a towering pile of mud-caked rocks to do her business. When she was done, she walked back in the direction in which she had come, but the path—along with Missy and Miles—was nowhere to be found. Gone.

Gone like Frank, her husband of 50 years—dead two summers ago of a "massive" heart attack, stricken at the wheel on the way home from the store. Fortunately, he didn't kill anyone as his car meandered off the road, wobbled over roots and rocks between two birch trees, down a mild incline, and into a calmly wandering brook. Gone like their sweet ol' collie Rufus not long before that—the sobbing goodbye at the veterinarian's table, the ride home choking on tears, the rear of the station wagon conspicuously untenanted, the smell of dog still infusing the upholstery. Gone like her youth.

But no, no time for self-pity now, and no more time for mourning. This was her "fresh start" after all, her "new life." After Frank had died, Jeannine found herself in a stretch of quiet stillness, waiting for the undertaker's other shoe to drop. Wives of a certain age follow their husbands down not long after, or so she'd been told (by, among others, supposedly well-meaning friends). So every day she'd waited for the terrible moment, the seizing up of her heart, the lump in her breast, the drooping face in the mirror. And thinking she'd soon be reunited with Frank under the loving gaze of God, she put her grief in a pretty package to be opened somewhere down the road if indeed there were further miles of road to travel.

Two years later, after yet another X-ray free of dark shadows and another good physical (decent cholesterol, middling blood pressure—*fit as a horse, healthy as a fiddle*, Dr. Michaud had said), she conceded that death was not in the offing, not yet. She was somewhat stout and tired easily, but she was healthy. She'd known then, standing on the sunbaked concrete of the Atlanta Health Center parking lot, staring out at the light glinting off the car windows, that she had a choice. She could open that package and give herself over to grief, tumble into its comfort like a pile of autumn leaves, or she could be one of those people she had always laughed at under her hand. Oh lord, no. Not that.

Not an "active senior."

Abrecan Geist and the Hilltown
Ten : an oral history /
by Anne Gare, et al. -- 1st ed. --
Leeds : Gare Occult, 1961.

(from Chapter 4: The Teenage Years)

A daguerreotype depicting a young man of fifteen years of age, Andrew Gass, who had by this point in his life retired his given name and taken on the moniker that would become notorious, Abrecan Geist. At fifteen, his face was covered with acne, and it spread across his cheeks and forehead, dotted the sides of his nose, and ringed his mouth, profuse especially at the corners. Overexposure muted the deformity in the picture; a blue tinge masked in part the worst of the matter. Otherwise, the boy has sharp yet delicate features, a strong jaw, a

Grecian nose, and wide-set eyes of a pleasing shape and aspect. He wears a gray sack coat and vest, dark trousers. His pose is that of defiance, right arm bent, long, delicate fingers resting lightly on his hip, left arm straight, hand in the pocket of his trousers.

It is a picture, to my mind, of the young man's struggle against his own vulnerability. He is trying to project strength and nonchalance, but in his eyes, I detect a pleading. For what? To be recognized? Admired? Maybe to be feared. Maybe I'm looking too deeply. Maybe he simply wants the terrible acne that desecrates his face to vanish. Maybe he thinks it never will.

The picture has another mark of significance: it is the first picture in which Geist's fingers are encircled with the two rings he had found in a box in his uncle's library—rings rumored to have been the original property of a powerful Beijing shaman, acquired by nefarious means.

It was not long after the picture was taken that the priests of Leeds began, one by one, to disappear.

The dots on the brightly glowing screen swirled, gray, small, and blinking one after another in turn. "Go," said Jeannine. "Oh, go, please."

No go.

A red exclamation point, like a long, bleeding slice above a puckered puncture wound, ringed by a circle of red. *Message failed to send,* read the text below the symbol. Jeannine thumbed the Try Again prompt and, wincing as if to forestall seeing the sad truth, glanced up at the power indicator: 40 percent. That didn't sound too bad, but Jeannine's phone was aging, just like her, and nearing obsolescence—just like her. Once you hit 30 percent, that number jumps down in devastating increments. 26. 18. 13. 4. A countdown to oblivion.

No go.

Message failed to send.

Try Again.

She walked a few feet forward, scanned the forest. Late afternoon sunlight shot down through sibilating leaves, creating shifting patterns over the dirt and the tree trunks and her hiking shoes, over her shockingly white legs, causing the blue veins to stand out in sharp relief. Birds chirped to one another. Unknown things chittered and rustled.

She called out, hating her own shrill intrusion into the soundscape, hating the weak and tremulous quality of her voice, the voice of an old lady. "Miles? Missy?" She called out again, louder, her voice breaking. Then she sat on a tree trunk and wept. She wept for Frank, for Rufus. She wept for Miles and Missy, no longer sweet children, and she wept for herself, a little old lady, indistinguishable from any other, except for the fact that soon her picture would appear in the daily: "Elderly Woman Found Dead." To be clucked over by people over coffee, shaking their heads, and going on with their lives. She stopped. Pulled herself together. *Walk in one direction,* she told herself. But which? She tried to discern the angle at which she'd come to the rock pile. Then she set off in that direction.

After Frank's death, to Jeannine's great reluctance, the kids insisted on her moving up north. True, their arguments were hard to oppose, for Frank had been Jeannine's life: he did the budget, house repairs, yard work, the cooking. He dispensed her medication and administered her eye drops. They had, over time, become a very insular couple. They didn't entertain, and they visited friends less and less, letting those friendships fall away. Jeannine had wanted for—and worried about—nothing, and in the absence of responsibility, she fell into a life of blissful ignorance and dreamy dependence. Now she would have to relearn self-sufficiency, even in mourning, and she dare not do that alone. In the end, she had acquiesced.

Living near Miles and Missy presented its own unique set of problems. They turned up on her doorstep when she wanted to be alone, insisting on "getting her out of the house," but were nowhere to be found on days when she was needy, when she wanted to talk about Frank with people who had known and loved him. And even on those dark, desolate days, she didn't want to intrude. They had lives all their own, after all, families to look after, friends their own age to spend their time with.

Miles did something in sales, but he couldn't explain what . . . well, he *did* explain it, but damned if Jeannine could make heads or tails of it. All that jargon. Like a foreign language. And Missy a dental hygienist, reaching into people's disgusting mouths. Jeannine had been a low-level insurance worker in Atlanta for the bulk of her life, starting out in the typing pool, back in the days when there were typing pools—ended up training every young soul who came in at the ground floor, acclimating them to the company and its ways, assigning them their duties. That was good, honest work, the tasks simple and straightforward. Not trying to get someone to part with their money. Not mucking about in other people's germs. You could feel at the end of the day as though you'd really *done* something.

Finally, she turned back the way she came. The decision was arbitrary, reached after too much time rooted in one spot, looking around her, listening for voices, for the calls of Missy and Miles, for the distant sound of traffic, the bark of a dog, the slamming of a door.

As she walked on, her joints just starting to ache, each gulp of air a little harder to attain, she found herself in a thicker section of wood where the trees stood closer together. She pushed her way through them, looking in vain for a path, and they seemed to get even closer together as she progressed. A few yards ahead, they were trunk to trunk, bark pushing against bark, a wall of gnarled and knotted wood. When she turned to return to the sparser wood, the forest still offered little in the way of passage. Eventually, all the trunks were mere inches apart in most places as if all the trees in the forest were swelling. Looking up, she saw the many branches intertwining, limbs overlapping limbs, the canopy of leaves thickening, blocking out what remained of the fading daylight. She fancied she could see the branches moving, reaching, growing into something like a spider's network of webs but with branches instead of silk thread.

Panic blossoming in her chest, Jeannine soon found she had to squeeze sideways to move through the impossible maze. Her progress was slow and difficult. Bark scraped her skin, and the stubs of branches tore at her clothing. It occurred to her that the forest might be helping her, forcing her onto a route that would lead to freedom. No. That was madness, a false hope. This is how she was going to die. Wedged among trees. Squashed. Whatever remained of her, whatever the animals . . . *slender* animals . . . didn't eat would be absorbed into the tree trunks. Gone. Never to be found, never to be retrieved. The forest would be one giant, thick tree, a wooden monolith—with whatever remained of her somewhere in the middle of the thing.

And now it seemed her fancy might come true. She'd gotten one leg between two trees, pushed her arm through, and her shoulder. Now her torso was stuck fast. She tried to move it back, to retreat, and couldn't manage to do even that. Her heart made woodpecker noises in her chest, and she felt the squeeze of asthma, of not being able to draw in air. She pulled back and pushed forward again and again and a third time . . . and she was out. Bruised probably and torn up definitely but out. She gulped in air.

A clearing stretched before her as if from out of nowhere, swathed in shadow, spruce blue in the long shadow of the treetops under a darkening sky strewn with soot-sotted clouds. A large, flat rock jutted into the clearing like a jagged dock over quiet waters. Turning, she saw that the forest behind her was wide open again, as normal. It was too early in her ordeal for her to be hallucinating. What had happened was *real*, despite what she saw now: an open forest, spaces between the trees, paths and rocks and roots. She climbed up onto the flat rock and sat, her white legs dangling over the edge, breathing in gulps of autumn air, fearing for her sanity.

She should look at her phone, she decided. Just a peek. She fetched it from her pocket and touched the button on the side: 36 percent now. Okay, not too bad. No reception still, but if she kept moving . . . she reached into her backpack and grabbed an energy bar. She had a heck of a time getting the packet open and was on the edge of tears when she finally managed to tear a small notch into the crimped edge of the packaging. She had no idea what people saw in these things. They were like stepped-on wads of chewing gum fashioned from stale oatmeal, and all they did was make you thirsty. Nonetheless, she took a few bites, her face an unconscious mimicry of a pouting infant, and took a pull from the last of her two water bottles. The warm water did little to slake her thirst, but it helped force the energy bar down.

As she lowered the bottle—mindful of saving water—she saw movement at the far edge of the clearing. The bushes shook slightly, and the wind ruffled the treetops. A large cloud sailed overhead, and just like *that*, twilight claimed the clearing. A shiver of fear shook Jeannine's spine, for she couldn't make sense of the form that emerged from the tree line. She dropped the water bottle and stared.

At first glance, it appeared to be a giant puppet of some kind, moving jerkily as though manipulated by an inexperienced handler. The joints in its legs were backward, giving it the appearance of some sort of mantis, but its surface—its skin, if you could call it that—was smooth, reflecting what little moonlight

shone from the edge of the dark cloud above. Its bald, maybe shaven head—
small, too small for its body, a doll's head on a giant—swiveled this way and
that. She couldn't make out its features. A smear of pale pink at the mouth, the
eyes and nose mottled by shadow. It crept along the edge of the wood, its head
bobbing slightly now as though sniffing something out. Jeannine became very
conscious of her perfume. ("Too much," Missy had said as they were leaving
the house.)

She carefully pushed herself up, swinging her legs over the edge of the rock
until she was on her side. She went to her knees. At this new angle, she saw that
the creature was stalking some crawling thing—something small and white
and lumpen—that bumbled through a patch of tall grass a few yards ahead of
it. She heard a thin wail as that of a terrified infant. Then it happened, quick
as a flash. A loose section of rock broke off under her hand, the sound echoing
like a cap gun shot. The thing's head whipped around, looking off somewhere to
Jeannine's right. Gossamer black wings unfolded like origami from its back. It
rose a few feet off the ground, wings buzzing. Its head swiveled . . . and stopped.
It saw her. And as the big, bright moon peeked out like a curious child from
the edge of the cloud, *she* saw *it*. She couldn't make sense of its face. It was that
of an elderly man—hollow cheeked, a toothless mouth, huge eyes like those of
a fly or a bumblebee. Then it flew right at her, its mouth a slack, elongated *O*,
its string-thin arms swimming, many fingers wriggling like the legs of a crane
fly. As the cloud reached out again to obscure the edge of the moon, Jeannine
scrambled backward and tumbled off the rock. A brief sensation of pain at the
back of her head, and consciousness fled her.

```
Abrecan Geist and the Hilltown
Ten : an oral history /
by Anne Gare, et al. -- 1st ed. --
Leeds : Gare Occult, 1961.
```

(from Chapter 4: The Teenage Years)

Meredith Spence (Former Classmate). We all heard about Father Godshalk of
Saint Mary's, about how William Well, out for his morning walk, had seen the
door to the rectory wide open on that chilly October day, dry leaves swooping

in and skittering around the bare floor, lighting on the bed and the modest desk, on the wooden chairs and in the stew pots. A single drop of blood on the walk and a doorframe slightly chipped near the bottom edge: that was the last trace anyone ever saw of him.

Then Father Marteau from the Edwards Church—his coach abandoned outside the Moody Tavern, door torn from its hinges, his horse wide-eyed and paralyzed with shock. There were no clues, only a long furrow in the mud and a solitary shoe. There was Father Shockley after that and Father Woodson. Father Grey. The last and the most brazen was Father . . . oh, what was his name? David Belding. They say he was taken from before a packed-full church house in the middle of mass. The door at the back of the church swung open, slamming against the wall, and a figure in a black sheet swept in along with a squall of snow. Before anyone could as much as drop their hymnals, the interloper had grabbed Belding by the neck and the belt and absconded with him through the door behind the altar. They searched the grounds and the woods beyond and found nothing. Not even a broken branch.

Jeannine awoke to the sound of voices, a man and a woman, not Missy and Miles but voices—the low drone of a man, the throaty, amused titter of a woman. *Saved! Saved!* She opened her mouth to call out but managed only a wordless croak. The weak, miserable sound of it struck her funny, and she wheezed and laughed, hardly any sound coming out. What a form she must cut: an old lady writhing slack jawed on the forest floor. When she recovered, she wiped the sleep from her eyes. All she could see was the mossy side of the rock. The memory of the night before struck her, and she touched her face, ran her hands through her hair, and brought them down into her range of vision, fearing her hands would be blood-soaked, that maybe she was brain-damaged, hallucinating. They were clean.

She endeavored to stand, not an easy task. Finally, she bent her legs, got her knees underneath her, grabbed the shelf-like edge of the large stone, and pulled herself upright. The field, which at night had been blue, proved now colorful with coral and yellow, a crowd of flowering plants waving an enthusiastic greeting to her in the wind. At the far edge of the field, almost exactly where she had spotted the mantis-like figure, stood a thinly bearded, tall man: his right hand—

large and flat—angled at his brow, his left clutched a gnarled walking stick. A
burlap shoulder bag hung at his hip. He was looking off Jeannine's right. At his
feet crouched a woman in frayed denim shorts and a flowing, yellow linen top,
her red hair in pigtails and her knees pink, tearing the flowers from the earth
and putting them in a red wheelbarrow with markings on the side that Jeannine
could not identify, though they looked vaguely Arabic with curls and swirls
but more elaborate, denser. It made her dizzy to look at them. Before she could
try to call out again, the woman spotted her and stood. Jeannine saw that she
was pregnant, far along too. The woman nudged her husband's leg and spoke
quietly, too quietly for Jeannine to hear, and they began to approach her. She
felt a touch of trepidation, mainly because of the young woman's initial reaction
upon spotting Jeannine: her face had briefly registered an expression Jeannine
would puzzle over for some time afterward. It looked like a confusing amalgam
of shock, shame, and anger. The strange part was that in there somewhere there
had also been relief.

"Can you help me? Do you . . .? I'm lost. I got separated from my children. Oh,
thank God you're here."

The man laughed, showing worn-down teeth and an expanse of gums, red
and chewed up, necrotic. A sharp, pungent odor wafted out, causing Jeannine
to take two steps back, her hand fluttering up to shield her mouth and nose in
involuntary defiance of a lifetime of deference and courtesy. "Certainly," he said.
"But let's not be rude dudes, yes? I presume you have a name?" He stretched
his bony, heavily veined right arm out to his right and then bent his wrist and
pointed back at himself. "I am Mister William Dither. Dither the Lucky, you
might call me, or just Lucky. Because the robust, Rubenesque, calli-*pyg*-ian
young minx directly to my left and wearing my ring around her fat little finger
is Missus Ellen Dither." The young woman blushed red but curtsied, her eyes
never leaving Jeannine's.

"*I'm* the lucky one," she said shyly, and Jeannine was shocked to see the young
woman lower her gaze directly to Dither's crotch and then back up to meet
Jeannine's gaze, at which point she winked with a lurid avidity.

"I'm . . . Jean-*nine*," she said, unable to keep the disgust from coloring her
voice.

"Why don't you walk with us? Our home is not far," Dither said. "We have the comfortablest couch in all of Leeds, in all of *Massachusetts*, I'd wager, and no sensible man would take that wager."

What else could she do? It occurred to her—she had no idea why it hadn't 'til now—to ask if they had a phone. But for no reason she could name, she was terrified to ask the question. Why? Fear of rebuke? Of some act of violence? She didn't know, but she did know that there was no way on earth she would ever ask. She would wait for them to bring it up. The woman went to fetch the wheelbarrow, and Dither muttered to himself as though alone. "An hour lost," she thought she heard him say somewhere in there. "Or two hours lost. On comes the frost, no hours to be lost, the cost, accost, holocaust, an hour lost . . ."

Ellen returned, nodded gravely, and the pair headed off toward the edge of the dark wood. Jeannine fell into step with them, Ellen pushing the wheelbarrow, Dither walking slightly behind her, his hands clasped behind his back, whistling tunelessly as he gazed at the clouds sailing across the sky. He reached into his shoulder bag and pulled out a blue thermos. He unscrewed the cap and drank. He looked at her, tilted his head like a dog, and grinned. He held the thermos out to her. "Oh!" she said. "My throat is so dry—are you sure it isn't a bother?"

"It's no bother at all, my dear, no skin off my bones." He handed her the thermos, and she drank. The fiery burn of warm, faintly carbonated alcohol tore down her throat and jumped up into her nostrils. She coughed and gagged, cried out. The man tittered, a high-pitched, mad sound, and gave her an exaggerated wink. "Oh, Will," Ellen said, laughter in her voice. "You're so bad."

Jeannine handed the bottle back to the man, speechless. And in doing so, she noticed something she hadn't seen before. There was a *hole* in his head, an inch above the center of his brow, puckered and slightly pinked at the edges, about the size of a dime. She tried to avert her gaze as waves of faintness washed over her. She was going to drop; she knew it. The world swam, rippling, distorting, curling at the edges. Through the vertigo, she somehow willed her legs to keep going, unaccountably embarrassed at the thought of telling them that she felt faint, that she was hallucinating (*was* she?)—the thought of admitting weakness. She'd almost rather pass out. She glanced over at Ellen who was walking a few feet to the left, half humming, half singing. She gasped.

Ellen was no longer pregnant.

In fact, she was as slender as the stem of a leaf. The world went orange, tilted just a little on its axis. Jeannine was all at once very conscious of the sounds of the group's footsteps in the high grass. But there was another sound, something like an animal darting to and fro in the underbrush around them. She felt something brush by her ankle, the brief but unmistakable feel of warm flesh. After a brief but intense internal debate, she cleared her throat and turned to address Ellen.

And Ellen was pregnant again, her hands on her large, round belly, fingers splayed. There was only the sound of the triumvirate's footsteps. A terrible notion occurred to her: what if these people themselves were a hallucination? What if she had been talking to the air, wandering through the grass, a madwoman in the last hour of her life? Jeannine went to her knees, gulped a few times, and fell unconscious in the grass.

Her dreams were vivid and lurid and bright. In one, she was a guest on a talk show with a garish blue set and a red-lit, cityscape backdrop. It was cold. She was seated in a guest's chair, wearing a paper hospital gown tied with a string at the back, far too short. She squeezed her heavy legs together, tugged at the hem, tried in vain to make herself smaller in the chair. The audience was a multicolored blur, the studio lights too bright for her to make them out. She squinted, hoping to see Missy and Miles in the seats. Next to her at his oak desk, the host—Will Dither dressed in doctor's scrubs, a stethoscope at his chest, grotesque mouth hidden behind a suspiciously brown-stained surgical mask—leaned in close and told her in an unctuous voice with a faint English accent that she looked terrific, even as she reared back in disgust.

Then the cameras turned toward her, and a red On Air sign lit up in the blackness behind the studio audience who began to applaud raucously. She held up her hand to filter the brightness of the lights and saw Frank, holding up a blood-spattered cue card. He was dressed in the blue suit she'd always hated, and his eyes were gone, gangrenous holes in their place. Silver smoke rose from them and dissipated as it approached the lights above.

Before she knew it, Dither had leapt up onto the desk. He was nude, though the stethoscope still dangled from his neck, swaying like a hypnotist's pendulum. Behind that swung Dither's grotesque, swollen genitalia. And he had become a spider, eight ropy arms propelling him across the desk, which was now a white-sheeted operating table. Frank was gone, and trees had burst from the floor where the studio audience had sat, the ruptured and splintered chairs adorning their branches. Hooded figures moved among those trees, holding lanterns high. Beyond them, beyond and above the trees, Jeannine saw the masts of great ships, heard men calling out one to another as echoing bells tolled.

Dither was on her in an instant. He held up his pinky finger in front of her face. It was tipped with a long, tapered black nail. He pressed its tip to her forehead, his face contorted by a terrible grin. It stung. As he inserted the tip, pain shooting its bolts through her cranium, he spoke again.

Nothing is happening, he said, his accent now German, his many hands gripping her shoulders, her arm, her wrists. A coldness entered her head, split her skull like a roofing nail forced into weather-worn wood. Her vision blurred, and her head swelled like a balloon. *Nothing is happening to you.* It was so soothing, his voice. So comforting. The tinge of menace faded as he repeated the phrase again and again, almost cooing. Her eyelids fluttered, and she felt the ghost of arousal billow at her groin.

nothing is happening to yooooou

She awoke to murmurs, laughter from another room. She was on her side, on a couch in a sparsely decorated, green-walled living room, her fists pressed up under her chin. An afghan of garish reds and yellows covered her. It smelled vaguely of mothballs. In front of her was a white-veined, onyx coffee table on which rested a steaming teacup, a black-tagged, black string hanging over the side. She caught a faint whiff of licorice and sulfur and wine.

On the walls were several posters in old wooden frames, the artwork itself faded: words, possibly old English, in swirls and curls, captioned artwork that depicted hooded figures, kneeling at elaborate altars; crude, antique-looking sketches of birds with dangling human feet, of winged infants, of laughing, winking heads impaled on the finials of an iron gate. A small, marble column sat in one corner, a widescreen television perched atop it. On the screen, multitudes danced, dirty and naked, shot from above by a camera that spun in widening circles, swooping and retreating, swooping and retreating. The strange, regimented, jerky movements of the dancing throng reminded Jeannine of Third Reich rallies. The sound, thankfully, was muted. In the opposite corner sat a high-backed chair, next to it a round table piled with books whose spines were frayed and torn. Jeannine rose quietly from the couch. The voices were coming from behind her, through an open doorway.

She walked to the window and pulled aside the red curtain to look outside.

A pergola with benches stood a few yards away, just across a tire-rutted, rock-strewn dirt road. Beyond that stood a curved row of cottages: some modern, squared off, all massive windows and right angles, others miniature Victorians, small bungalows, A-frame structures. Beyond those towered a wall of leafless trees.

"Our little enclave."

Dither's voice, just behind her.

"Welcome to Laurel Woods. As old as Leeds. Maybe older." He began to recite, his voice bouncing along: "Its first inhabitant, a nameless man who heard thunder and feared it not. Who walked in utter darkness and did not cringe at the sounds in the caves and in the trees. Who reached before him not with trembling fingers but with fists. Who did not tremble and clench but strode mightily. Who saw other creatures and other men and thought only of subjugation, of control, of brute fulfillment and flesh laid bare for the biting or else cooked and consumed, both acts of fury and joy. He breathed in smoke and spat coal."

Somewhere behind them rose a whirring sound, loud.

"Join us in the kitchen?"

```
Abrecan Geist and the Hilltown
Ten : an oral history /
by Anne Gare, et al. -- 1st ed. --
Leeds : Gare Occult, 1961.
```

(from Chapter 4: The Teenage Years)

Raymond Dwight. This isn't largely known (laughs). That's what you call understatement. I may be the only one left who knows about it. And there's certainly no one left who can verify it from firsthand knowledge.

My father told me about it when he was in his cups. He was among the constabulary who responded when word came of the abomination, the sacrilege that had occurred in the church house on Withering Farms Road. I'm an old man now, far older than my father was when he took me to the fire-lit study and told me exactly what he'd seen. I'm an old man, death tapping at the window, and my father is decades in his wooden coffin that probably still reeks of whisky, but I remember his account even now just as he told it to me, the candlelight flickering in his spectacles, his large hands clenched into fists.

The church, the oldest in Leeds, in Western Massachusetts in fact, consisted of eight pews situated around a central aisle. At the front, a raised platform bore an altar and a podium from which to address the congregants. The priests were sat two to a pew, each at either end. Their eyes had been removed. Candles had been pushed into the eye sockets, most of them lit, illuminating the clouds of flies that swarmed and buzzed. Their mouths had been wrenched open—jaws broken, lips ruptured—jammed full of communion bread. Their hands were nailed together at their chests. In their laps sat open bibles, smeared with fluids of unknown origin and defaced with charcoal graffiti. Father cursed himself later for not checking to see whether the bibles were open to any particular passages. They were all too stunned at the appalling blasphemy. The work of Satan if there ever was a Satan. My father never believed in God, but after that day, he sure believed in the devil. He took to drink even more than before. Killed him before long.

The eyes? They were found the next day in the collection basket.

Meredith Spence. The priests were never found. Did we suspect Abrecan? I can't say that we did. He seemed to smile to himself a lot when it was talked about. But he was a gentle boy. That he could have, on his own, kidnapped at least six priests and somehow got rid of the bodies? No, it didn't make any kind of sense at all.

Ellen stood at the granite counter, her hands gripping a club-like pestle, grinding something in a cracked stone mortar. To her left, among a few cylindrical spice jars, a tall, narrow blender howled, a pinkish tornado churning within. Queued up next to the blender was a phalanx of thermoses and a small pile of lids. At her feet, looking out of place in the black-and-white tiled kitchen, sat the red wheelbarrow, half full of flowers. Ellen was barefoot, one knee pressed up against the side of the counter for leverage, toes curled tightly, grunting as she worked. Jeannine noted her large, taut belly pressed firmly against the counter's edge. Will crossed behind her and sat at the table where a smoking pipe rested in an ornately carved wooden stand, curling paths of smoke intertwining above it. Jeannine stayed in the doorway, looking around the room for a telephone, finding none. She looked at Dither. His eyes went unfocused, and then semi-transparent inner eyelids, like those of a cat, swept across them. He sunk slightly in the chair and exhaled mightily. His head tilted, and the tip of his tongue appeared between his lips.

"Is he out?" asked Ellen.

"I'm sorry?" said Jeannine.

Ellen snapped at her: "Out. *Out* like out cold, fucked off?"

Jeannine said, "Well, how in creation am I supposed to know? He looks asleep!"

Ellen, muttering curses and invectives, dug her hand—her dirty, unwashed hand, Jeannine noted—into the mortar and scooped out a sopping mass of grayish gunk with tinges and swaths of coral and yellow. She strode over, gripped Dither by the shoulder, and smeared the stuff across his forehead, using her index finger to jam some of it into the puckered wound. Jeannine suppressed a gag as Ellen swirled the finger around, pushed it in deep, thrust it in and out. A rank odor assailed her nostrils.

A movement at the wound now, a fluttering shadow, and then a fat, bloated leech wriggled its way out. Its wings unglued themselves from its side as it climbed onto the slight ridge of Dither's brow and started to flutter and blur, shaking off the dampness. The leech launched itself into the air and rose to the ceiling where it bumped its back repeatedly as it explored the cobweb-strewn corners of the room. Dither's inner eyelids pulled away like curtains opening, and he chuckled and grinned as he wiped the gray discharge from the wound, which now looked red and irritated. He scratched at its edges with the long, curved nail of his pinky finger. The winged leech lighted on a thick nail that jutted from the brick wall, just above the window, and began to groom itself like a fly with its string-like front legs. Occasionally it squawked a staticky outburst. Then it fell to the floor with a wet thud, dead.

Dither leaned back in his chair. His inner eyelids opened and closed, his mouth went slack, and he began to vocalize. Ellen dropped the pestle and went around behind him, putting her hands on his shoulders. He stretched out his legs as far as they would go. She sang along with him, and his voice separated from hers, rose into a wordless stream of syllables. Another leech poked its head from his wound and fell out onto his lap, and then they were falling out of the man's head one after the other in seemingly inexhaustible numbers, filling the air in the room with their cicada-like buzz and the metallic, putrescent odor of their impending deaths.

"And here we go again," Jeannine said out loud as her back slid down the doorframe and consciousness fled her once more. This time, there were no dreams. She jolted awake with a dull pain in her tailbone and the stirrings of what was likely to be a terrible migraine. The light in the kitchen was the same, as though no time had passed. But the blender was clean, the wheelbarrow absent, the thermoses lidded and stacked among the spice jars. To her considerable relief—for she could, if she strained to do so, imagine the last few minutes of a dream—there were no leeches on the floor and no traces of any in the room at all. Dither and Ellen were seated at the table. Before them lay a small figure, something human but gnarled and pallid. Jeannine stood shakily and approached the table.

It was a boy—or most of a boy—with bruised and scarred stumps for legs. Pre-adolescent, maybe seven or eight, a small, perfectly formed nose, wide-set blue eyes of brilliant kaleidoscopic array. His hair was up and unruly. A small torso, protruding belly, arms . . . but the left arm was adult-sized, long. Jeannine gasped: it was a prosthetic arm. The boy raised it over his head and brought it down to his side. He belched a bubbling, high-pitched laugh. A flash of panic hit his eyes, and he gulped a few times as though fearful of vomiting. Tears welled.

"What is this?" she demanded.

The couple just stared at her, expressions inscrutable.

Jeannine addressed the boy, speaking loudly: "Are Will and Ellen your dad and mom?"

He shook his head no, brought his right hand—his real hand—up to his eyes. He dug his knuckles into one eye, then the other. Jeannine feared he might bruise himself, so fiercely did he push his fist into his eye sockets.

Then he pulled his hand away. His eyes were clear and bright but inexplicably now devoid of intelligence, blank like the painted eyes of a department store dummy. "I have no parents," the boy recited in a strange, wobbling baritone. "I have no past. I am a soldier in the service of truth."

A flash came to Jeannine. A story in the *Gazette*, the sun's rays hitting the newspaper where it had sat next to her breakfast plate. "Missing Boy." She'd only glanced at the story, but she remembered it because the boy's father's name was Miles, though *her* Miles had never seen fit to give her a grandson. What was his mother's name? Linda? Laura? Lucy! No . . . Lucia!

"Son," she said, "Is Miles your father? Is your mother Lucia?"

Somewhere in the eyes, a flicker.

"They must miss you terribly."

"I have n-no pare-parents. *No* paren . . . I am a . . . no past . . . a sol-soldier." The boy's teeth began to chatter.

"I'm taking you out of here," Jeannine said. "Do you understand?"

A movement, maybe just a shiver, maybe a slight nod. Close enough. She lifted the boy into her embrace as Dither and Ellen looked on. His prosthetic arm stuck out straight past her neck. The warmth of him, the thrum of his skin at her touch. She dared not wonder how long it had been since he'd been held, touched with a parent's love. She pulled back and looked at his face. His eyes were squeezed shut, his brow knit in some mix of relief and confusion.

"Don't you even hold them, you nasty little people?" she said.

Will and Ellen looked at each other and smiled. Will squeezed Ellen's hand.

"I'm taking this boy, and we're leaving. You will drive us out of here or point the way to the main road. If there's any evidence at all that he was . . . was *violated . . .*"

No reaction from the pair, which might be good.

"I'm going back to my children, and he's going back to his parents."

"Of course," said Will. His smile was wide, his eyes gleaming. Then his brow furrowed, and his tone darkened. "Of course," he said, "there's no road out . . ."

The boy tightened his grip on Jeannine's neck. "Shhhhh, now," she whispered. "Shhhhh. Are you hungry, dear?" He nodded against her neck. "You bring him something to eat," she commanded Ellen who turned briskly and exited the room. And something for me while you're at it. I can't believe you haven't offered me anything to eat. Unreal."

Dither stood, beaming.

Jeannine ignored him. How dare they treat a child like this. How dare they. Not only a child. Children. She was certain of it. There were more. That moth-like creature brought them here to be disfigured somehow, inducted into . . . into *something.*

Soldiers.

She couldn't leave them here like this, untouched, neglected.

She couldn't leave.

After a meal of lamb stew and steaming bread, the couple showed her to a modest bedroom with a quilt-covered bed, bare walls, and a small nightstand, adjacent to the room where the boy slept. She fell into an uneasy sleep in which she kept picturing the trees hemming her in, layers of leaves and branches blocking out the sky in increments. Sometime later, she was jolted into full, startled wakefulness. She didn't know what had caused her eyes to jump open, but her heart thumped fast and loud in her chest.

A vision gripped her, fully formed, a movie in her mind, garishly colored like photographs in old cookbooks: the boy, standing in a field, a glinting chef's knife gripped in the hand of his prosthetic arm, the arm whirling around in its socket like the rotor blade of a windmill. Over the horizon, a phalanx of children come, some on long prosthetic legs, some without jaws, all armed with blades and sledgehammers and shears. In this vision, she freezes as the boy approaches, something off, something wrong and unnatural in his eyes. The blade goes up into her stomach, and the boy's eyes lock with hers. For a second, she almost *feels* it, the cold intrusion slicing upward through bowel and intestine, a horrific feeling of *displacement* and bright, blinding pain.

She rose from her bed and looked underneath. Her backpack sat in the shadows like a sleeping animal. She grabbed it and tiptoed across the room to try the door. To her surprise, it was unlocked. A curve of light emanated from under the door of the boy's room. As she walked noiselessly past, she heard from under it a kind of grunting—in amusement maybe, or pain. Maybe masturbatory, she thought, her ears going red. Then a sick little chuckle, right at the door. She somehow refrained from shrieking but hastened her steps.

In the moonlit kitchen now, she moves on instinct. A thermos goes into her bag. The spices follow, the clinking thankfully muffled. Her breath comes in short, sighing bursts. Guilt assails her: what is she, a common shoplifter? A thief? Why is she taking this risk? Proof? She doesn't know. All she knows is that her addled, confused brain is insisting she do it. Who is she to argue?

The lights come on behind her, and her body stiffens. It's over, she thinks. She turns, expecting fully to see the boy, the knife in his faux fist, or the couple, advancing in rage, but instead she faces the podium of the Look Diner, behind which a grinning blonde hostess stands. She looks behind her and sees the double doors of the diner, herself reflected in a half crouch, dark circles under her wide eyes. She straightens herself up and looks back at the hostess, who grabs a menu from a wooden pocket on the side of the stand. "Just you tonight?" she says.

In the Blade's Wake

If your eyes are unwell, your body will be shot through with darkness. If even the light within you is darkness, how black that darkness must be.

A MAN KNEELS ON RED AND SCARRED KNEES BEFORE A SMALL FIRE IN a sparsely furnished basement bunker. His shadow roams the ceiling above him, warping and stretching and whipping itself about, splitting into two, into four, now five. He is stripped to the waist, sinewy, no skin to spare. Constellations of skin tags pepper his torso like brown rocks breaking the surface of sand. A rash like a squall of pink-red clouds paints his left side from armpit to hip. He wraps his arms tightly around his torso, takes a deep breath, and leans forward until his face is inches from the flames. His lashes curl in the shimmering heat. His nose and cheeks go bright red. Blisters bloom on his brow like time-lapse flowers. His lips whiten and then brown. He holds his position until his lips begin to blacken and peel, and he leans back, his singed lips moving in silent prayer, tears pouring down his cheeks. Still kneeling, his torso falls slowly backward. His shoulder blades and the back of his head touch the concrete floor, and he sleeps.

Sometime later, he rises like a puppet pulled up slowly by its strings. His face is expressionless and slack, his eyes dead, teeth pressed tightly together. He raises his arms slowly until they point upward, splays his fingers. Shivers wrack his form. A seizure? A squall of exultation? We do not know, and we do not know if *he* knows. He slows and then stills. He bends at the waist, his fingers brushing the floor. He is breathing heavily, almost panting. Legs trembling, he walks over to a pile of clothing in the corner. He dresses: faded jeans worn white at the knees, a crumpled black T-shirt, gray hooded sweatshirt, seam torn at the underarm. He slides his feet into bargain-rack sneakers, also gray, once white.

The year is 1990. The man, whose real name he has labored to forget but who has renamed himself Jabin, has streaks of white hair above his ears and in the whorl of hair at his right eye. Wrinkles crowd around his eyes, bracket his mouth. His teeth, dull and chipped at the edges, point this way and that, overlap as though massing at a locked door demanding exit. The man is twenty years old. He looks twice that age.

He climbs a small set of wooden steps that lead from the windowless shelter into the abandoned church, slides past graffiti-strewn pews, slips out the side door.

(excerpt from the childhood notebooks of Andrew Gass)

The blains and boils on my skin I chose to wear proudly, for I came to see the condition as a physical manifestation of exactly that which I aspired to be—an abomination before god. A fuck-you to nature. A refutation of, or a rebellion against, beauty. For beauty is widely (and mistakenly) thought to signify Godliness and Virtue when to my observation it often masked Cravenness and Guile. I began to think of the blemishes—even now I think this of my lasting scars—as the very language of blasphemy etched upon my face. When I turned my face to heaven, I told myself, angels hissed and turned away, cherubs took wing, coal-black turds tumbling from their backsides, Christ turned away to face the cross upon which he was nailed, God himself gulped and gasped like a fish pulled from the ocean.

Jabin walks the streets of Leeds. Girls arm in arm laughing, girls walking alone, their packs bouncing at their sides, intrepid faces. Hair tied up or cascading down over their shoulders. Angel faces, hard faces, baby faces. Men leering or loitering in groups, raucous laughter, shoving. Beasts, all of them, abject and wretched, dripping in sin. Godless at best. Anti-God, surely, some of them. Now having crossed some nebulous border, Jabin is in the town's skid row. Cigarette butts curl in the sidewalk cracks, and crumpled lottery tickets lay pushed into the mud along the curb. Garages and laundromats and junk shops and package stores. Garbage bags torn open, spilling their insides onto the crumbling walk in front of the tenements. Nerve-rotted ghosts, ejected nearly a decade earlier from the state hospitals, linger pale and filthy against light poles or sprawl on benches blanketed in graffiti and discarded coats. Sometimes they hassle or follow wayward tourists or tussle in broken-glass alleys, spitting obscenities. Later the police will come, all tight frowns and unveiled venom, to drag them off—the familiar choreography, men spun around and pushed against cars, slammed to the pavement, the percussion of shoes scrambling on concrete. These are lost people, angry men and women, pushing back against their diseases, against chemicals, against instincts burned into them by dissolute or drink-sotted fathers and mothers. They're harmless or at least only harmful on a small scale. They are not the devils of the city.

Jabin has heard the *real* Leeds devils. He heard them from afar as a boy, heard them even more clearly recently from the speaker of the transistor radio he used to keep in the nave: their voices, their unholy choirs, their searing wails. The dented speaker spewed strange, unholy music, sinister whispering, the monologues of the damned and the brain-wrecked. It told of the obscene and monstrous appetites of Pope Sevenius, of the wicked treachery of the warlock Abrecan Geist, of children dragged from their homes and transformed, devoured, or sacrificed to Sevenius in unspeakable rites. He was drawn to the radio like an addict to a blue flame under a blackened spoon until he began to fear for his soul and his salvation. He finally doused the radio in kerosene and set it alight. Even after the old transistor was reduced to a smoking lump with a singed, cracked antenna, it whispered to him. Its insinuating, salacious voice assailed his ears all the way to the Mill River, where he brought it one hot, stultifying summer day, and into which he threw it as hard and as far as he could. He had watched until the bubbles stopped. Ash still remained in the crevices of his hand and would not come out no matter how fiercely he washed them.

These devils are *here*, all around him. A terrible thing to know. They live in towering, dark-windowed houses that line streets that reach like long, curling fingers into the woods, in well-appointed condominiums above the posher shops; others dwell in the dense wood that surrounds the curving, climbing roads of the hill towns, in terrible tall houses, in disused diner cars, squat cottages, farmhouses at the crests of hills, rusted-out trailers embraced by creeping foliage and many-fingered grasping vines. They are selectmen, shop owners, men in suits and men in oriental robes, in police uniforms, in old-style suits and hats. They convene at the Bluebonnet Diner, in the basement of the Grouse Bar & Grill, in the private rooms of the posh and pricy Fern and Olive. They convene in the heart of the woods or at Anne Gare's bookshop. In those unholy places, they hold their Sabbaths and perform their unspeakable rituals and rites.

The bookshop looms ahead now, throwing its shadow like a cloak over the walk. He should leave, he knows. Not just leave this street. Quit the diner. Flee from the town. Start afresh somewhere else. Follow his faith like a fleeing lover— track her down and land her and fold himself into the soft white grottos of her tresses.

If he hasn't now, he never will. He has to go in, has to see for himself the festering fulcrum of the city's darkness. A voice tells him he is here for a purpose. He used to be convinced the voice wasn't his own.

The shop is situated between a tobacconist and a pizza parlor in a two-story, brick commercial block. A table out front displays a variety of dog-eared westerns and pulp paperbacks. Rows of floor-to-ceiling shelves, sun-faded mass markets in the window display, the page edges yellowed. He crosses himself, drawing snickers from a band of pre-teens in halter tops and tight jeans. Persecution and ridicule: he is used to it by now. He looks up at the city clock at the top of its tall tower. He has time. Heart pounding, he stands before the door. He mutters, "If it must be, I offer my body as a living sacrifice." He pushes open the door and enters the shop.

A bell heralds his arrival. Standing behind the counter as though having risen to greet him is a brown-haired woman, arms at her sides as though in a trance. At first, seeing the lank hair and the gaunt chin, the wiry arms, the man mistakes her for the notorious Anne Gare who founded the store, but she disappeared ages ago and would be at least a century old, not in her forties like this woman. She reaches up and pulls her hair from her face, and to his substantial relief, it does not bear the terrible deformity that rendered Gare's face a horror. No, it is the unremarkable, plain face of a woman a bit too thin, face hardened, pale, almost nonexistent lips, nose an afterthought.

He nods a hello, trying and failing to keep from his face a look of moral disgust, disgust tinged with fear. He casually flips through Technicolor cookbooks—beef loaves wrapped in bright-brown bacon, plump roast pigeons, pies with garish red cherries like pustules under decorative doughy lattice—all the while terribly aware of the nearby stairs to the basement. The notorious basement of Anne Gare's, and anyone could just stroll right in. He wanders over to the fiction section, picks up a book at random. He flips through it, pretending to read. The counter woman is seated now, stroking a long-haired ginger cat with squinty eyes. The cat purrs with a slight whistle. Jabin shelves the book, takes a deep breath, and descends the stairs into the basement. Books are piled against the wall on each step, on the landing. He stands at the archway at the bottom of the stairs and surveys the room. Faded oriental carpets and three aisles of dust-strewn shelves. He walks down the center aisle, glancing left, glancing right. Religion and Spirituality. Death and Dying. Film and Television.

Voices murmur from the far end of the basement. Something about their tone, an echoing distortion, sends a chill up Jabin's spine and into his brain. Words flutter in his ears, just outside the borders of his comprehension. His skull goes to ice. Now scuffling and a thump or two, a high-pitched snigger. Then silence. Jabin exits the aisle into an open area. Beyond another wide archway, low shelves line the back of the room, above which portraits of men— and one of Gare as well, hair covering her face—glare down at a great oak table surrounded by pulled-back yoke-crest chairs. Books lay spread open across the table among strewn papers covered in inky scribbles. He approaches to examine the books and papers but stops short.

Whispers surround him like the beating wings of moths, and the shop goes frigid. Jabin shivers in the cold; his teeth clack. The tips of his fingers go numb. The lights flicker and dim. A bulb pops. Now the room goes hot like the flick of a switch. His ears burn, and his neck dampens with perspiration. It drips from his hairline down through his eyebrows. It gets into his lashes. He wipes it away, his temples pulsing with migraine, nausea unfolding like a great black umbrella in his gut. He reaches out to pull one of the papers closer to him, and his hand begins to tremble and then to seize up, his fingers starting to bend backward.

One of them breaks, the sound like a pencil snapping in two. He turns and flees. As he gets farther from the table, the nausea fades, the room cools, pain leaves his hand. He hits the stairs at a near gallop. The woman still sits, now asleep, the cat a curled-up bun in her lap. She is as still as a cadaver. The cat hisses as he passes, swipes at the air in his wake, claws out like curled spikes.

The Geist observations and homilies / by Anne Gare and Rexroth Slaughton -- 1st ed. -- Leeds : Gare Occult, 1971.

Was God the Invention of Man? *He was a man-made god, yes, but not solely man-made. Man conjured him from dust and dead skin and elixirs of unknown provenance. And so god was born into a universe, and Man told god that universe was his creation: he was a confused god, a frightened god, a fake-it-'til-you-make-it god who never quite made it. It was enough to make a god go mad, and that it did, for he was sufficiently insane to convince Man to summon up a devil. I am an heir of that devil.*

And now we have church spires like middle fingers raised at every community, a million gimcrack Christs on a million meaningless crosses, their faces screwed up in a shadow of agony—I call it a shadow because Christ knew nothing of the real, raw agonies that afflict mere human beings. Put a nail through my hand but let me keep the ones I love. Suspend me from wood but provide me enough of a lifetime to do all I want to do. Unbind my hands from your scratchy twine of rules and restrictions.

Christianity! That blood-spangled, many-fingered lie! It is a religion of abjection and insecurity, attributing all failures to the lowly Self and all victories abetted by the so-named lord. Irony of ironies, even that lord is insecure, demanding worship and self-abasement under punishment of eternal torment. Torment that slanders the devil who wants no part of inflicting physical pain on the no-longer physical being.

And watch the Christians and judge them by their actions. Watch them strut and preen, warmed by the glow of their own moral disapproval like a bishop basking in his own farts in a sealed confessional.

To hell, I say, with cringing Christians and ass-in-the-air Arabs.

Bring me in tethers that lunatic god who does not know that he wants me to kill him, but he does, and I am loath to turn him away.

Even as a boy with another name, Jabin had been aware of the town's sickness. Though his parents had painted shut his windows, he could still hear the surrounding neighbors in the sleepy suburb, playing their radios loudly into the night. The sounds emanated from numerous dim-lit windows: he couldn't hear the words specifically but murmuring voices, tuneless music, sounds that he could not identify. Weeping, shrieking, ululating, preaching. The shadows of the plastic animals in his mobile warped and stretched, prowling the ceiling like slithery demons. The night sky changed colors, the clouds dancing strangely, the very moon like a carbuncle, extravasating fluids into space, holes forming in the firmament, the stars clustering and clotting in those holes.

He knew about the disappearances too, boys and girls. Jeremy Scheer, for one—Jabin could still see the kindergarten class picture as though it were right in front of him, Jeremy's chubby pink face, huge grin ringed by a blonde bowl cut. Kimberly Sandham a few years later. The Bantam girl, what was her name? Range-el? Rang-el? He noted also, though not consciously at first, the propensity of townsfolk to bear an abundance of children. Three- and four-seat strollers in Look Park. High chairs stacked in restaurant corners, a disproportionate number of baby goods shops on Main Street. Beleaguered young parents with small armies of toddlers in tow. He was the rare only child. Was Leeds just an . . . overly fertile place?

His parents warned him young. Stay away from the woods. No radios in the house. If you take to an Abrahamic religion, don't attend services in Leeds— drive the extra few miles to one of the surrounding towns. The police are to be avoided. Don't do anything to draw attention to yourself, especially when you are old enough to drive. Avoid clusters of strangely dressed old men in odd places. He had seen them too, by the dumpster behind the auto-repair shop, in the tick-strewn field next to the motel, the field that collected fast-food wrappers and empty baggies and plastic shopping bags tied to fences like coded messages.

In his teens, he prayed to God. He knelt at the side of his bed, a Pooh bear in a red shirt staring brainlessly at him as he pled for forgiveness. After he got his driver's license, he would drive to the Catholic church in Florence, the next town over, kneeling, standing, sitting, nodding his head and mouthing the words as the priest performed the Catholic mass at the feet of a despondent Jesus, arms outstretched, eyes rolled heavenward, his sight surely impeded by the thorns of his crown jabbing at the sky in search of more heads to bloody. He remembered hearing the Lord speak to him, guiding him out of the paths of temptation—of flesh, of reward on earth, of opulence. The Lord's voice was calming, loving, clear, ageless.

He couldn't remember when the voice spoke for the last time. It had fallen silent so many years back. *And so,* he had thought after a time, *it must be that I am where I need to be. For now, I am not in need of guidance. I am on the path to salvation, original sin behind me, paradise ahead.* But after a time, that silence was supplanted by . . . he never knew quite how to describe it . . . by a malevolence that tainted the very air. The sound of the wind, the twittering of birds, the omnipresent moan of car engines and human chatter—it all seemed to mock him. *They are all blocking the Lord's voice,* he had thought, but even in his silent room with sealed windows and locked door, the very silence laughed at him.

Your God is dead or fled.

Those words awakened him one night, just preceding his rising from unconsciousness, propelling him back into the world. He could still hear the voice echo in his room. He cried out, and just on the other side of the sound of his voice, he heard another voice say something, but he did not hear what it was. He gasped and clamped his hands over his mouth, but even that voice was now gone. He was alone. He feared opening his door, for what if it opened into an abyss of nothing and he pitched forward into it? Shivering and weeping, he waited. At some point, he fell backward into sleep again and did not wake until daylight had filled his room.

When he went outside, he encountered a city altered. Over the next few days, with mounting horror, he marked the changes. St. Elizabeth's on Royal Street replaced the beckoning stone Jesus, which had stood tall on its lawn, with a great crow, wings outstretched. The wooden Christ in the Edwards Church had been inverted, his fallen robe obscuring his face and leaving him obscenely exposed, a pool of blood painted beneath him on the floor. The remaining crucifixes and crosses in the town? Gone. Even in the jewelry and trinket stores, not a cross to be found. The devils had taken a step forward, hastened their steps toward stealing the hearts of holy men.

Not long after, Jabin clocked in for his shift at the Look Diner where he had started working at the age of sixteen, where he would work his whole life, where he would die staring up at the blurring ceiling tiles. From the morning into the afternoon, he labored over the hot griddle, plating pancakes and hash, eggs over hard, burgers and fries, liver and onions for the old cranks who cackle at the counter and decry politicians local and global, who bitch about gas prices and joke about getting away from the wife. He fell into a trance, the chatter and the clacking forks and the waitresses and the sizzling grill all fading away, his outer being reading the slips, cracking eggs one-handed, while inside he recited the Lord's Prayer before a stately, cloth-covered altar, over and over again. Slips of psalms and songs were next on the playlist "Holy, holy, holy Lord, God of power and might . . ." Before he knew it, his shift was over, and he was standing in the break room slipping his arms into his jacket. He showered at the YMCA on Prospect Sheet, a gray-tiled room with gray-rubber curtains. Sometimes he's in there for over an hour, head bent, the water washing over him. He lets his mind go blank.

He woke that night, pushed the stained sheet from his body. He thought of Adam, of Adam's seed, carrying sin as blood carries a virus, as a man carries a bomb suitcase, as a radio wave spreads a pernicious idea to lodge in the souls of all whose ears it enters. Sin passes from Adam to all of man, he mused—it is transmitted, poison in the ear, an injection into the arm—yet it does not dilute nor does it weaken. Indeed, it grows stronger, fouler, crueler. It poisons all: babies are born screaming into the world, carriers, distributors, their seed, even at that beginning stage, readying itself for the eventual quickening. Sons and daughters of dereliction, mutinous whelps. Jabin feels this sepsis crowd around him every day. It bubbles on the lips of men, roils in their guts. It is in him too; this he despises most. He pushes it out from his pores, prays it out. But it's in him, in his spine, wound around his veins. Grace is the antidote, the way to salvation, but grace is elusive. Like God's voice, it's gone, gone, gone. He writhed in turmoil, ignoring the erection that strained until it breached the window at the front his underwear. As he fell back to sleep, he ejaculated into the sheets, his midsection thrumming. He gasped and fell the rest of the way into blackness.

The next morning, he entered Anne Gare's bookshop for the first time.

2016. In the intervening years, Jabin prayed and worked and watched. He built up his body at the YMCA, strengthening his arms, getting his heart going, and he built up his mind in the library. He read sacred texts, profane texts, the lives of saints, and the chronicles of the depraved and debased. The Bible and *The Magus.* The Koran and *The Secret Doctrine.* The Upanishads and *The Kybalion.* He would be called to service, he knew. He hoped he would be prepared.

It happens now in the quiet annex of the Forbes Library. Jabin opens a copy of the famed *Libellus Vox Larvae,* and a slip of paper sits at its hinge. An address scrawled in smeared ink. An illustration of a complex symbol of swirling lines and arrows.

Jabin walks by the bookshop now on his way to the address on the slip of paper. It is dark inside. A sign on the window reads "Closed Until Further Notice—Family Emergency." He turns down a side street, houses set back from the road, bracketed by fence or hedge, windows staring impassively over. Now, a street where the houses are spread out farther with a forest for a backdrop, and between two massive, rolling lawns, he sees the L-shaped office building set off from the road, framed out front by bushes trimmed into perfect rectangles and in back by a denser, impenetrable wall of woods. Aside the pristine front walk, a stone obelisk lain on its side displays the street number in raised, stylized digits. He enters through blue-tinted-glass double doors into a long hall with off-white walls, a patternless tan carpet, and a tile ceiling with fluorescent lights. Distant murmurs, the tap tap tap of typewriter keys, the rhythmic whine of a photocopier. Green, numbered doors with names in white lettering on brown tiles. Garrett. Pilcher. Cozine and Cobb. He stops at an unmarked door with no knob, no visible means of access. He crosses himself and knocks.

The door opens to reveal not a waiting room nor an office but what appears to be a motel room lit by the flickering bluish glow of a television. Browned and chipped mini-blinds cover two smallish windows. Though it's bright outside, no light comes through the windows. It's as if they look out on a black wall. On a sagging, stained bed at the far end sit two thin men with drooping flaps for cheeks, bare, narrow chests, bulging eyes, their noses just glops of squished putty. Both wear only faded denim cutoffs. Their bellies hang like banners over their belts. They must be either twins or victims of the same disfiguring malady. The one on the left has his gaze fixed on the television, which sits on a precariously leaning cart; it's broadcasting a colonoscopy, the camera pulling back slowly through a fleshy, fold-ridged tunnel. The other weakly raises an arm to beckon him in. The man's upper arm flab, shot through with blue veins, swings like a grotesque flag.

Jabin takes a few steps forward. Movement to his right grabs his attention. Standing atop a small armchair is a child of maybe four, clad in a small brown suit with a fat tie. An over-large, Halloween-store wig, a blond-bob style, perches atop his head. His ears jut out like side-view mirrors. His face is obscured by the shadow of the wig, but one of the men on the bed strikes a match, and Jabin gasps aloud. The face is featureless, an oblong peeled egg with neither indentation nor protrusion. Scrawled on the gray-white skin in ballpoint is a childish attempt at eyes, one sitting slightly higher than the other, a down-pointing arrow for a nose, and a scribbled cloud for a mouth. A small hole in the boy's neck reveals a nest of malformed teeth. He raises a swollen hand and wiggles three fat fingers at Jabin, and the tiny mouth babbles a high-pitched fusillade of nonsense syllables. When it finishes its shrill monologue, a bubble of mucous forms at the aperture. It swells and pops softly.

The man on the bed reluctantly pulls his attention from the screen. With some effort, he raises himself off the bed. His counterpart swings his legs up and falls promptly to sleep; his snores tear through the room like ordnance. The standing man kneels by the bed, retrieves an oblong black box. He lifts the lid and tilts the box toward Jabin.

In the box sits a large chef's knife. Engraved on the blade is a series of logograms and odd symbols. Jabin approaches, tilts his head. *May I examine it?* The man nods, and Jabin notes with a start that the pupils of his eyes resemble those of a goat and that the veins that spread over the sclera are a nauseous green. He turns his attention to the knife, lifts it gingerly from the indentation in the box. It has surprising heft. He grips the handle and finds that the balance is perfect. He examines the partial bolster, the broadness of the heel. He runs the blade gently across his thumb. A white line lay in the blade's wake. A bead of blood squeezes through it, rests like a small gleaming berry on the skin.

The man pulls a ragged, crumpled cloth from his pocket and proffers it to Jabin who refuses it, wipes his bloodied thumb on his pant leg. The man raises his eyebrows. *Does it suit you?* Jabin nods, returns the knife to its box, takes it from the man, and in turn, he pulls from his pocket a wad of cash and hands it over. "Go in Christ," the man says.

Jabin glances at the television. Illuminated by the light of the camera, a grinning gray face rises from the depths of the colon toward the surface of the screen. Its lips are blue, its eyes ravenous. The faceless child, still standing on the chair, begins to ululate, a rising falsetto, shrill and jarring. Jabin flees.

Back to the church. His heart slows. He examines the knife again. He does not yet know what it is for, only that he will need it. He opens the curtain behind the altar and slides in the box.

That night, Jabin slept, and the darkness of sleep opened like a great black door, admitting him once again into Anne Gare Books. He was back in 1990. Anne Gare dangled by a frayed rope tied around a light fixture behind the register, her neck grotesquely elongated and bruised. Flies swarmed around her head in a humming murmuration. The flesh of her taut legs was torn away in great bloody swaths, revealing wooden bones at which termites chewed loudly. Her blackened eyelids fluttered and opened, revealing bulging eyes—little pink lizard tongues darting out from under the lids, licking at her eyeballs. She hissed at him like a cat with her fat red tongue. Flecks of spittle landed along the counter, bored holes in the wood, causing thin streams of smoke to climb toward the ceiling. Jabin averted his eyes and descended the stairs to the basement. Sound seemed muted, so he lowered his head and shook it. A feeling of *loosening* and then loose detritus in his ears. He dug with his fingertips, pulled away clumps of reddish-brown earwax. As he dug further, pulled out more, sounds flooded in: the Satanic call of the flies, the wet, squelching mouths of the termites, the distant hiss of acidic saliva eating away at the counter upstairs, the piped-in music, a wobbling noise like the spinning of a large top about to come to rest.

Details stood out that he had not noticed the first time around. All stood stark and clear as though Jabin had put on glasses for the first time, never having known his vision was impaired. Chairs stood here and there among the stacks, old wooden chairs mostly, the occasional discontinued office chair, its faux-leather skin ruptured, revealing yellow foam innards. A box fan's casement rocked atop a low shelf, its whirring broad blades gray with accumulated dust.

Just before the archway, a phalanx of plastic bins huddled under a spot where the ceiling was darkened and discolored and peeled.

Jabin sits. He arranges the papers before him, examines the books: elaborate sketches, maps and coordinates, arrows, numbers, some kind of pictographic language—or several different languages—all surrounded by ink spatter like black stars. At the center of one paper, a date: twenty-eight years in the future, circled numerous times. Under that, in huge, ink-clotted letters: **LOOK**. The books appear to be mostly about the resurrection of the dead and the tools required for resurrection rituals, such as talismans, rings, powders, and totems. One illustration depicts a man hovering in rippling air, arms and legs akimbo, hissing angels fleeing, men and women below among broken dishes and scattered scraps of food, their mouths agape, hands at their ears. Blood streams from their eyes.

Voices float around the room, originally unheard back in 1990, now surging in and fading out like a radio signal just out of geographical range.

"... *his dreams* ... *permeate* ... *all shall inhabit* ... *sentient shadows, frantic air, laughing soil* ... *caper in green flame.*"

"... *we humbly obsecrate—instauration, Geist drew* ... *dust and tincture, H-ring and loop* ..."

"*One torn man shall bring the body—another hast the rings—and the old woman with the herbs and seeds and ceremonial powders* ... *gather* ... *great repast* ..."

"*One hundred years plus forty.*"

"... *two lifetimes* ... *patience* ..."

That date ... twenty years in the future. Consciousness finds Jabin, and for a moment, he is in two places at once, two times. He rises to the surface of 2016. That date, the circled date, is next year. A year from tonight. He sinks back to 1990 and then forward a year ... he hears voices chattering, the clinking of silverware on glass, aromas floating past him, spices, charred meat, car exhaust, sulfur ... Windex?

In a flash, Jabin knows what is to happen and knows that God has chosen him to stop it.

2017. Jabin woke early on that propitious morning, surprised that sleep had somehow found and claimed him. He rose, washed, and stepped out to watch the city awaken. Everything was freighted with menace. Black clouds with shimmering red hulls lolled in the sky. Windows opened their yellow eyes in the apartments above the stores. Squirrels chased one another up and down a tarry telephone pole riddled with staples while below a man in an oversized coat dug through a trash barrel. Jabin sat on the stone steps outside the shuttered chocolate shop and pulled from his pocket a penknife. Wincing, he traced the bulging veins in his wrist and arm. Then he jammed the blade into the crook of his elbow and stifled a scream. As the blood welled up, he offered a prayer to the silent sky.

Anxiety bloomed in his stomach and spread out into his limbs. Tonight was the night. He thought of the big knife. He thought of blood and resurrection and a world molded to the dark vision of an undead warlock, humanity trapped in a lethal unreality.

Jabin let the water wash over his body, tilted his head back so that it pooled in his eyes, ran down in rivulets on either side of his nose. He tasted the water as it ran over his lips, winced a little at the sting.

He shut off the water and wrapped a towel around his waist. In the locker room, he dressed. The place was deserted, he noted—strange as he'd arrived to the general chaos of the open swim, children and parents chattering, old folks stepping into their bathing suits. He strode through the empty lobby, past the unmanned receptionist's desk. He pushed open the door to leave, and there was no parking lot. He was in the middle of a rural road. He turned to look behind him, and the building was gone too, the road stretching back and curving away, disappearing into the trees.

He was being kept away from the Look. This he knew . . . but he didn't know how to stop it. He slapped at his face, screamed as loudly as he could. Squeezed his eyes shut and opened them. He felt foolish, standing in the middle of the road, having what must have looked like a tantrum.

Looked like to whom?

He pushed away the thought, regarded the silent houses on either side of him, the windows reflecting the leaves. The road was familiar to Jabin somehow, but he couldn't quite place it.

The only way out, he'd been told many a time, *is through.*

He began to walk.

About a quarter mile from where the YMCA had stood (and then had vanished), a car sat running in the middle of the road. It looked like his first car in fact, bought for him by his father when he'd turned seventeen—a white Pinto wagon with wood-panel sides. He remembered the absurd model name: the Country Squire. It was running. The driver door stood open.

Jabin approached cautiously, calling out. As he rounded the back of the vehicle, he saw the car was empty. He got in, eased his back into the seat. It felt like coming home. He put the car in gear and drove.

The road unspooled before him, seemingly endless—no sign of shops or gas stations, just houses, shuttered and still. He happened to glance at a garrison colonial house that had in its front yard a giant inflatable turkey, partially deflated, in a gold-buckled pilgrim hat, deranged eyes set over a drooping yellow beak, flattened wattle sunken partway into its puffed chest. A few miles down the road, he slammed on the brakes, his mouth falling open. The same house, the same sunken turkey. He stared for a time. The house and the turkey stared back. Jabin blinked. He pulled away and drove, keeping an eye on the houses on his side of the road . . . watching . . . watching . . . and *there*, the *same house*, the same partially collapsed turkey. He wrenched the wheel, jerked the car over 'til the passenger-side tires climbed the curb, and then clambered out without putting it into park. He approached the turkey as the car meandered back onto the road, drifted a few yards, and fluttered like a half-screwed-in lightbulb, like a bad television signal, and blinked out of existence. He crossed the road, a blurred blue Toyota still as a cadaver to his right and, above him, birds perched frozen on the telephone wire, beaks pointing this way and that.

Silence and stillness. Paralysis. Like walking through a still picture. Jabin jabbed at the turkey with the tip of his boot and stepped down, pushing the plastic into the soft earth beneath. A whistle sang, high and shrill: escaping air.

And the world came alive.

As though a great, ghostly hand had spun some celestial volume dial, in came the whooshing of air, birdsong, and treetop thrashing. Then an unusual sound. Ordnance, crack . . . crack . . . crack crack . . . coming closer, louder, faster. Just beyond the house, the trees began to bend as though gut shot and dissolved to dust, billowing and raining to the ground, and then he saw it, coming slowly around from behind the house—a great cadaverous face almost as tall as the house itself, its eyes fixed and dilated, nostrils flared, lips thin and white with dead skin, parted slightly, revealing a row of gray teeth like scuffed stone. Its hair hung lank. The face morphed into a great brown watery wave, carrying wriggling, living earth in its many foaming hands, and then back to that terrible dead face. There was no God in it, no indication that a soul had abandoned it. *It was always thus.* The mouth opened. Jabin backed up and turned to run.

He was running at full bore when his shadow left the ground at a right angle, rising up as if to block his path. He skidded to a stop. The world before him was flat, his shadow expanding, extending over the reach of the trees, darkening the sky. He reached out, touched what should have been a distant tree. Canvas, rough and dimpled against his palm. He ran his hand up, caressed the dry, rough sky. He fumbled in his pocket, frequently looking behind him at the looming, approaching face. He found his pocketknife and cut a line down the canvas. He parted the slit and looked in. His jaw dropped, and the color went from his face. *Such beauty . . . such interminable beauty.* Lights played on his face, and sweet music fluttered around his ears. For just a moment, as he peered through the slit in the canvas, his expression was the mirror of that of the looming face behind him—the face of a man tempted by sin.

Then the devil, taking Him up on a high mountain, showed Him all the kingdoms of the world in a moment of time. And the devil said to Him, "All this authority, I will give You, and their glory; for this has been delivered to me, and I give it to whomever I wish. Therefore, if You will worship before me, all will be Yours."

He cast his eyes away, and it came to him. He *had* to get to the Look. And there would be only one way. He turned and ran at the looming face. As he approached, the eyes came alive, blood vessels like red threads, forming strange shapes in the whites, the nostrils flaring, the mouth opening into a cadaverous grin. Just as the two were about to collide, Jabin leapt up, hooked his hands over the bottom row of teeth—pain in his palms and the eye-stinging odor of halitosis—and he climbed up onto the dry dead tongue and dove into the dark hole of the throat.

Abrecan Geist dream dictionary and atlas /
by Anne Gare and Burton Stallhearse --
1st ed. -- Leeds : Gare Occult, 1966.

(from the original series of handmade pamphlets, 1900–1950)

1900. *With the fading of the acne that so scorched and disfigured my face came new dreams.*

I daresay that throughout my teens I never dreamed at all. The dreams I'd had as a boy of that terrible manikin with its knowing eyes had been enough for a lifetime, I surmised, and I would spend the rest of my days awake or asleep and never again in that in-between place where the unreal becomes real. Oh, I spent a surfeit of restless nights, twisting my sheets in my fists, changing my position by the minute, held helpless by my unresting imagination, refighting long-resolved arguments with adversaries, putting pictures in my head of lush harems, of great battles, bodies rent and blown open with swords, maces, cannonballs, leaving tattered bodies in their wake as they bounced like ebullient ghosts through battlefields blanketed in fog. But these were my images, wrought consciously, often as fodder for fevered masturbation. Over countless nights without sleep, I conceived of a city of concrete and steel, bisected by rivers teeming with blood-borne boats fashioned from the bones of impossible beasts, formed maps and charts, constructed tall buildings and shacks and mansions, compiled statistics. I created beings as well, from a pantheon of demons down to the mundane: clerks, importers, clothiers, tobacconists, drifters. I gave them wives industrious or lazy, children rambunctious or reserved, as I saw fit. These existed nowhere but in my head, yet I swore I could count on their consistency.

So it was with no small measure of fear that in the very first dream of my adult life—now in my own bed in a grand house bequeathed to me by my aunt and uncle, furnished and staffed by way of the inheritance they had put aside for me—I happened upon my own city in the deepest part of the forest. I knew it at once by the stanchions that marked the city line; like the talon-tipped hands of an angel, they rose from the earth to greet me, to welcome me into my own creation. Instead of entering, I stumbled, fell backward onto my bottom on the damp, branch-strewn forest floor. Over the stanchions, I spied church spires and great towers, all of which were straight from my teenage night work. I did not enter, for I knew all too well the creatures and devils with which I had populated this dream-city. Through this dream, the aromas of food—butter and beef, the sharp tang of bacon. I woke drooling like a dog who needs putting down.

I did not log this dream.

By the next night, I had been gripped by an insistent ague. I desperately gathered the bedclothes around me to quell my shivering and shoved and kicked them away, only to have my sweat turn cold and chill my body once again. The darkness pressed against me like gelatin, but when I lit the lamp, the light stung like a score of scorpions.

Somehow, despite the discomforts that took turns assailing my poor body, I fell away to sleep. I saw my mother towering—head shaved and sunken—above my bed, seizing and retching. I saw great bats with bare, swollen bellies—surely pregnant with spiders—fluttering around my chamber. I saw the ceiling's skin peel away to reveal a complex system of large, glass pipes through which bubbling pinkish liquid propelled segmented, white-skinned creatures with folds of fat that resembled swollen gills. In my hysteria, I cried out, and one of the terrible things rolled around to regard me, three pink-rimmed eyes—pupils like malformed stars—opening in its bulbous, topmost segment. Its mouth opened too, and it was a horror.

I woke sometime later, my fever breaking as I blinked my way into the daylight that filled my room. The sweat poured out of me in a great flood, all at once, and my throat and nasal passages cleared. I became aware that my servants were toiling all about me. The ceiling had been torn open and lay in pieces on the floor. Any electrical wires and pipes had been removed, and I could see straight through to the floorboards of the attic. Servants, countenances set and grim, moved this way and that, hauling buckets, pushing around mops. I lifted myself out of the sweat-soaked bedclothes and looked down at the floor. In a dank little puddle with pink bubbles around its edges lay a mottled swatch of white flesh, and near that, a little marble floated. It rolled in the liquid and looked up at me, a popped-out eye with a pupil like a malformed star.

Reader, the house was not constructed with a system of glass pipes, and such creatures did not exist. I had dreamed them into being. And if I could learn the discipline to control what I dreamed, there would be no limits to the changes I could make to the world.

Jabin landed hard in the seat of a city bus. People around eyed him with a vague, disinterested curiosity and went back to studying the landscape or the smears on the windows or the insistent colors of their phone screens. The bus pulled to the side of the road, and the doors opened. Jabin stood and on shaking legs made his way to the doors, hopped down to the curb, and sat in the brown grass. The diner stood before him. It looked different somehow. A creature with a wrap-around, half-lidded eye and a vertical glass mouth. Jabin looked at his watch. His shift was to start in five minutes.

Fear gripped him, followed swiftly by despair. He had forgotten the knife.

Deaspersion

THE FIRST DEATH OF ABRECAN GEIST. ABRECAN GEIST LAY ON THE great oak refectory table in the alcove of the basement of Anne Gare's bookshop. On shelves and sills, forty-eight blue flames shimmied over the trembling wicks of forty-eight bubbling candles. The great man's face gleamed with perspiration, his eyes rolling wildly in swollen sockets. He gasped, sighed, opened his mouth as if to speak, and then closed it again, unable. He bared his brown teeth. Even in the dim, flickering candlelight, his jaundice was remarkable, and he looked like a sarcophagus of amber in which some shapeless demon writhed in restless slumber. Shadows separated from the walls, shadows with eyes—the ghosts of the colonial dead. Their fluid faces undulated, stretched, and slackened, warped, zigzagged, and dilated. Their groans formed a dissonant, unholy choir backed by the fiendish drone of buzzing flies.

Anne Gare flew about the room like a great fluttering bat, her frayed dress trailing like an army of vipers. All the words from all the books in the room pried themselves from the paper and slid out from between the pages, forming thin ribbons that circled around her narrow frame. A man with a paunch like an overstuffed pillow sat at the outer edge of an old wing chair: a great old suitcase at his side, his face in his hands, a snaky vein in his balding dome pulsing, his snow-and-gravel beard tangled and pink from spilt wine. Geist's eyes found his, and they stared, each helpless, each unable to help the other.

The hot breath of the demonic dead—such nauseating stench!—intensified until the mirrors began to warp and melt, to depict indistinct horrors in their darkly shadowed depths. Light bulbs burst to powder, and shelves wilted and crumpled like saturated cardboard. Hell felt close.

With a tremendous tearing sound, the ceiling sprung from its moorings. It rose with a force stronger than gravity, pancaking the upper floors—the bookstore and a two-story apartment, all of the contents flattened—and the whole mess spiraled up into the clouds. The books, now bereft of their words, leapt from the shelves and followed like a mad murmuration of starlings. They penetrated the black clouds, and lightning bolts shot out, curled up like serpents, and rolled themselves into flickering, pulsating orbs that darted this way and that. Each time the orbs hit the underside of a cloud, the cloud began to melt, sending black tendrils down the sky like ink running down a gray wall.

A Philco rolltop radio, sitting atop a low shelf, spat an explosive squall of static. Its dial brightened, glowing a gauzy green, and its volume knob began to rotate, faster now, still faster, and Geist's voice, strong and loud, called out from the speaker. Gare and the man turned to face the radio. Gare knelt and held out her open hands toward the speaker as if to clutch the voice and hustle it away down the sunny avenues that surely still existed upstairs. *I have dreamed a new Leeds,* Geist's disembodied voice said, and on the table, Geist's pupils shrunk to the size of mites. *And when you bring me back, that new Leeds shall become the world, and the world shall become that new Leeds. Where the sun is afraid to show its yellow face! Where clouds gather to cloak the dark deeds of dream-bound men! Where the unafraid man is free from the shackles of peace! Free to beat down the boss, the bible-man, the agent of the Federal Communications Commission! Leeds shall become the world. And the world shall become Leeds! Where even the earth and the sky are not to be trusted by men who fear, where the senses shatter at what they behold. Surreality will reign, the fetters of the dreamer—me!—will fall away. Insanity will hold sway, and the insane will be as gods. Syndication,* it cried. *Syndication!*

The static rose like a strengthening storm, like the roar of approaching oblivion, obscuring Geist's voice.

Geist inhaled. Everything drew closer to him. His eyes bulged and went bloody red. His tongue stuck out, long and taut and blue. A rib cracked in his chest. Then another.

Then he fell flat. The blue of his eyes faded like the colors in a sun-aged snapshot. "Bring me back," he said, his voice now a trembling whisper. "I don't want to go."

And he exhaled his last.

And then he was gone.

All fell silent. The room cooled and darkened. A wind perfumed with the aromas of spring swept through. The man in the wing chair raised his head. His face and eyes were pink and wet. Anne Gare knelt, her forehead on the floor, and wept—ugly and loud and whooping. The man joined in. Finally, she quieted. Then she gathered her tresses and rose. In a blue-veined fist, she gripped a knife with a wide blade. She rolled Geist onto his stomach and began her work. The man, still weeping, climbed the stairs slowly and carefully like a man sick from alcohol, lugging the case at his side. When he finally attained the front walk, he turned and looked at the blank space where the shop and the apartment used to be, at the sheared off brick, the bruised and blemished sky.

Sirens began to sing their wailing song in rounds. "Hurry," he called to Anne. But she and the body of Geist were already gone. He hastened himself away too, the case in hand, Gare's words replaying in his memory. *Walter, take with you the dummy-body, the rings, the powders. Hide them in the dreams of the dreamers of Leeds, in their secret dream-places, the precincts of sleep. When the time comes, the dreamers will bring them to the appointed place. Do this in memory of Andrew.* Behind them, whatever remained of Geist dreamed the shop and the apartment back to life. All was as it had been. The books on the shelves. The shop with its cash register and stool. The apartment with its furniture and its secret closets and its portraits and curtains and tapestries. Then something else changed. An absence swept through the block, a billowing sadness. The people in the neighboring apartments woke and wept: all of their hope, all of their prospects vanished, and they knew not why. Despondence and despair held sway. Geist was gone.

Jeannine sat at her table, the menu unopened and unread in front of her. She had ordered, was waiting for her food, but had no memory of what she ordered or for that matter how she'd gotten here. This is how it starts, she thought. The fog of senility. She scanned the room for Missy and Miles. What if they were here, but she no longer recognized them? How would she get home? She had no idea how to go about getting a taxi. No, think. You can just ask the hostess. She'd call. She glanced out the window. Will Dither was dancing and capering in the woodchip-

*strewn landscaping among the azaleas and petunias and begonias beyond the
window, a satanic grin spread across his face. And his . . . his penis was hanging
from his unzipped pants, a swollen, pulsing thing with the head of a cobra. The
cobra head looked at her with shining black eyes, like teddy-bear eyes, and its
pink tongue flickered. A waitress walked by and matter-of-factly drew the blinds
as if this was just a nuisance, a normal occurrence, and then swept away toward
the coffee pots. Someone at another table belched extravagantly, and she turned
to see if she could locate the perpetrator. She could not. Looking back at the
table, she was surprised to find a massive rack of ribs before her, a pile of mashed
potatoes shored up against it like buttery ballast. Also, as a nod to greenery, a
sprig of parsley curled up like a caterpillar. Next to the plate, a prim cup of tea,
steam rising from its surface. This was what she'd ordered? She laughed out loud,
causing a man with a mustache and feathered hair to jump, nearly spilling his ice
water. She was surprised to find herself suddenly starving. She dug into the ribs.*

Walter Clough, all of ten years old, ten and a half actually, though he considered
himself too old to acknowledge half-years in the count, sat hunched in the
church pew, all but ignoring the proceedings of the christening going on at the
top of the aisle. After having tired himself out studying the necks and hairstyles
of a variety of distant relatives and well-wishers, he now cast his gaze at the
array of stained-glass windows, depicting bearded men in colorful tunics and
who loitered in various unknowable scenes and formations, heads encased in
strange futuristic glass globes, inscrutable but somehow alarming expressions
on their faces.

He found them nakedly terrifying, and he frowned with the unhappy
certainty that they would make their way into his dreams: their weirdly
pointed joints like those of puppets, thin arms and legs swinging ominously
in slow motion. He leaned over toward his mother who, strangely, leaned
away as though reacting to some unpleasant odor. Walter stored that away to
contemplate later. "Who are those men," he whispered, pointing at the windows.

"*Shhhhh.*" Walter noted that no one reacted to his whisper, but his mother's
hiss made a few heads swerve their way, recriminations in their eyes.

The priest must have cracked some sort of joke then as the participants in the
christening tittered loudly, causing the infant to begin to fuss, which transitioned

into a series of disconsolate shrieks. The priest feigned admonishment and said a few hurried, dissembling words to the close family. And then commenced, to Walter's profound relief, the rustling of coats and retrieving of purses and belongings.

Walter's mother grabbed a handful of his jacket shoulder and yanked him upward. The two joined the rest of the group exiting the church into a heavy downpour, the trees and the houses blurring and bending behind the rain. Walter decided he would try again.

"Who were those men?"

"I'm trying to concentrate here," she said, stretching her neck to peer at a bent street sign. "Three lefts, two rights, another left," she said to herself.

He waited until the look of distracted concentration left her face, and he tried again. "The men in the window."

"Walter." This was almost a growl, and it told Walter the conversation was over. He looked out the window and brooded. Church had bored him to tears, and the reception would certainly be as boring if not more so, lost in a sea of incomprehensible adult conversation, and . . . dread settled into his belly . . . kids who he just *knew* would dislike him instinctively—his thick glasses and his fat little belly and his unkempt hair. Shame mixed with the dread. Why hadn't he combed his hair? Why couldn't his mom afford better clothes for him instead of these flea-market things, stretched out and shapeless and still smelling of attic and mothballs? And as the capper, this oversized gray suit jacket, which matched nothing else.

By the time they reached the house at which the reception was to be held, the rain had all but stopped, and shafts of light dissipated and diffused the storm clouds. The tall house itself, gray-shingled and four-storied, ringed in the back by towering trees, stood in a dramatic cone of sunlight, and it seemed to be somehow more real, more there, than all that surrounded it.

The two bypassed the porch, Walter's mother's hand clutching the bunched back of his jacket, and circumnavigated an array of shrubbery sheared into squares to find a canopy-covered array of round tables fronted by a long table piled with gifts in ribbon-strangled boxes. Along the side of the house, atop a row of cloth-covered tables, Sterno-heated water pans sent up plumes of steam, awaiting food trays. Underneath in ice buckets were beer bottles, colored in off-putting browns and greens. He hoped their hosts had thought to supply the festivities with Kool-Aid or something similar as he watched a trio of little girls engaged in some very serious discussion that appeared to have to do with a doll's house whose front half stood opened like double doors, revealing intricately appointed interior rooms with little tables, couches, chairs, and chandeliers.

"Find a seat, Son," Walter's mother said, barely looking at him. "Mommy needs to pee." And with that, she hurried around to the back of the house.

Walter scanned the tables. Most of the seats were already taken by bouffant-topped women in dresses of yellow and emerald green and sapphire blue and by neat-haired men in linen suits. Intimidating. Alien even. He dreaded the thought of the bubbly, interminable interrogation that usually came when he was without his mother in the presence of adults. He could already feel his face going red at the process. Then he spotted a table at which only one man sat, blue eyes staring out over the tops of sunglasses. Walter couldn't remember having seen him at the church. The man wore a pressed white shirt with dagger-sharp collars under a diamond-patterned black-and-gold vest. His sleeves were rolled up to just below the elbow. A scuffed silver medallion rested at his neck. His hair was gray-black, swept up over his ears. He looked like someone from another era—flashy but somehow serious, possibly dangerous. Walter felt a strange and unprecedented pull. The man was surveying the other guests, his expression—nearly a sneer—suggesting strongly that he knew something unsavory about each of them. Walter's anxiety forgotten, he wound a path among the tables and pulled back a chair directly across from the man. He sat.

If anyone would know the answer to his question, this man would.

"Who were the men," he said. "In the church windows?"

The man's eyes focused, found Walter, and warmed. "You're absolutely right," he said. "No need for any perfunctory introductions. Right down to the meat of the matter. The men pictured in the stained-glass windows are called the a-*pahst*-les. Do you know what *apostle* means? No? It means 'one who is sent away.'" Walter, who had on more than one occasion been sent away by his mother, nodded gravely. "These were missionaries—in other words, pushers. Nudges. Gossips and liars. They were a kind of entourage for Christ. His publicity department."

The man's eyes narrowed. "Someone bullies you."

Walter thought of Jimmy Sitch at school. He nodded.

"And that bully has people who follow him around? Who back him up by repeating what he says? Who tell stories about him to inspire fear and deference?"

"Yes," Walter said, picturing the cruelty that warped their faces and made them monsters.

"I'll tell you a secret. The boy and his followers are considered by their community to be 'good Christians.'"

Walter mulled this over.

"Oh," the man said. "Food."

This confused Walter for a brief moment until he followed the man's gaze and saw the line of caterers in white suits and black aprons march forth from around the back of the house, holding trays out in front of them in gloved hands as though presenting offerings to a hungry god. Great gobbets of red meat with charred skin in a bloody puddle; a choppy ocean of mashed potatoes, shards of red skin here and there like the sails of half-sunken boats; a field of wilted, wet greens; parsley-littered, hacked-off chicken legs and wings stacked in a generous pile; slabs of white fish sprinkled with spices in a shallow, cloudy pond; fists of cauliflower punching up through a field of broccoli florets. Walter's mom trailed them, her gait unsteady. She held a bottle of champagne tightly by the neck. The man looked at Walter and smiled. "I don't think you're entirely given over to Christianity yet, are you. You haven't been 'confirmed.'" What a word that is. So redolent of the world of *business*.

"You've heard the church's pitch today, and you're about to hear mine. You are just at the cusp of a very vulnerable age—open to influences. You are weak but with a tremendous potential for strength. And it appears that your household might suffer from a lack of strong guidance. If I have anything to say about it, you will not be one of those people who credit God for their successes and shoulder the blame for their failures. Let's load up our plates, shall we? I think we have a lot to talk about."

Walter followed the man over to the back of the just-forming queue, his head swimming. He fought a mad urge to take the man's hand. Instead, the man took his and beamed down at him. *Father,* thought Walter.

Dave Strell leaned back from the table and struggled back to full consciousness. He had eaten in a post-traumatic haze . . . and apparently an unfettered frenzy. The savaged carcass of the chicken sat in a puddle of cola. Cola-soaked napkins

and bones lay scattered across the table, broken and splintered, with bits of skin dangling from them like fired-upon flags after a battle. Chicken skin clung to his fingers like damp tissue paper, and bits of it were wedged under his nails. He felt gristle between his teeth, and the burn of acid indigestion shot knives up through his torso. He belched more loudly than he would ever have done in public before the world had gone screwy. This brought a little relief, made him feel almost human again. A cracking sound outside caught his attention, and he sat up a little to see Randy Jerry, a fire extinguisher jutting from the front of his head like a fat red horn. Blood flowed from his wound, waterfalling down his face. He lapped at it with his tongue, and then he spotted Dave and roared with rage, beating his chest like an ape, stomping in the woodchips, sending dirt and cigarette butts flying up into the air around him. Dave ducked back down. He had a sense that Jerry wouldn't come into the diner, not in that condition. But he, Dave, dare not go out there. The waitress approached, her order pad in her hand. Her glance fell to the mess on the table, and her brow raised slightly and settled. Dave admired her customer service skills. She'd be great at office work, he thought. "Anything else, hon?" she said.

"Pie," said Dave. "Cherry pie.

"And more napkins."

```
Abrecan Geist and the Hilltown
Ten : an oral history /
by Anne Gare, et al. -- 1st ed. --
Leeds : Gare Occult, 1961.
```

Anne Gare. The years of Geist's twenties and middle thirties, prior to the formation of the Hilltown Ten, would not by any assessment be termed "well documented." This is not due to a lack of activity nor a lack of people willing, if not eager, to discuss his travels and his work and his doings; rather, it is by design. Restraint is required of us, his biographers. Some things are best kept obscure.

We can allow that, besides honing his skills as a practitioner of his own form of black magic, he read as much on the topic as he could (though he would reject most of the philosophies he encountered) and kept notes on the books and papers that so absorbed him. He read Blavatsky ("dense and dull") and Glanvill's *Saducismus Triumphatus* ("accidentally made appealing that which he attempted to excoriate"). He devoured Levi and Waite, Lenormant and Spence, and de Plancy's *Dictionnaire Infernel* whose pages were mostly loose, if not detached, from overuse, as was Trowbridge's biography of Cagliostro.

Of contemporary occultists, Geist was most ill-disposed to Crowley, especially having read of his (rumored) penchant for cat killing. One should, even upon accidentally causing pain to a cat, apologize and prostrate oneself in the desire for forgiveness. For cats are familiars and allies, possessed of strong wills and a profound connection to the mystical and the ineffable and not mere sacrifices, certainly not a thing to be tortured. It turned Geist's stomach. It was an insult. Not wicked but craven. Apologists denied the act had ever occurred; Geist rejected them out of hand. He also found pathetic Crowley's addiction, for it evinced powerlessness and betrayal of the "will" the man was always on about—what Beast, after all, would suffer a helpless allegiance to a chemical? It was tantamount to faith, to obsequiousness, to *worship*.

He read Crowley's works wincingly, crossing out passages with such vigor that he shredded the pages, so obtuse and dense he found the man's writing, the only bursts of coherence consisting of juvenile stabs at philosophy with scrambled and re-worked words of his betters, sprinkled with mystic nonsense and numerology and yoga. Crowley was no Agrippa. Though Geist grudgingly admired the former man's sartorial style—it might be said with only small fear of reprisal that Geist mimicked it—and he was good for a tossed-off bon mot or quotable quote.

Geist despised Crowley much in the way that you and I feel a natural revulsion to those similar to us. Granted, the similarities between the two men were superficial and mainly physical—in bearing, height, bulk, and in their fiery glares there was an undeniable superficial resemblance. Geist was no mountain-climber (he has been quoted as saying that he'd have difficulty reaching the apex of the tiniest hillock), but he did once have an excruciating attack of photokeratitis that mirrored that of the so-called Great Beast, an affliction for which to seek relief the former alternated between a cold compress and having Anne Gare weep into his eyes. Also, like Crowley, Geist considered himself a poet and tried his hand at fiction with varying degrees of success.

What follows is an excerpt from one of Geist's more autobiographical, yet obviously fancified, short stories, one that might lend some insight into his communing with Anne Gare and others in the notorious Hilltown Ten.

About the great wizard, who went by the name Grim Features, rumors swiftly swirled through the mouths and ears of the townsfolk: that he kept as a familiar a great anteater who knew and could speak sixteen words in English (and four in French); that he abstained from food and drink for a period of six months with no deleterious effects and thereby attained a higher level of consciousness; that his first meal after his fast consisted of a soft-boiled egg and a fried oyster, chased down with moonshine; that the scar across his forehead was the result of his splitting open his flesh and skull (without anesthesia nor alcohol) to examine his own brain, on which he performed a delicate form of acupuncture in order to gain untold insights; that he recorded his snores at night and sold them at great cost to a demoniac translator and the result was his most moving poetry.

Some of these were true and some not. For an example of one of the latter, he had gotten the scar on his forehead by a simple fall on an icy staircase. Of course, the stairs were indoors in his chateau, whose temperature at the time was 75 degrees, and it was also summertime.

Another rumor was halfway true, that Grim Features had, in his youth, committed grave acts of violence and was extraordinarily unpredictable and dangerous. The former was undeniably accurate, for as a teenager, he had committed a series of murders, which had been part of a larger ritual whose ends were a little more sophisticated than simple mayhem but which would have been impossible for investigators and the constabulary to comprehend. As to the latter, Features was not a naturally violent nor volatile person himself, though among his retinue of researchers, chefs, acolytes, and hangers-on there did reside the odd murderer whom he might put to use in extreme cases or in cases where all magic had failed. At the time of our tale, he was but young and between his time of killing and his time of having perfected magic. His reputation, though specious and fictitious, aided him in times of conflict, even if he did not at the time know why his enemies used cautions that often rendered their attacks on him ineffective.

He had seen the woman at the edge of the wood, trapped by some unknown force presumably, for she never breached the tree line nor did she retreat farther than a few yards into the trees. A pair of blood-sotted wings lay at her feet. Her face was void of features yet somehow managed, maybe due to how shadows fell across it, to convey desperation. He made it a point to pass by that way more often. Fear kept him from approaching her, fear that whatever held her fast might also ensnare him. So he studied on the matter. He consulted his book of spells, his drawer of hawthorn and snake root and stranger, alien things. After three hundred and thirty-three days of cloistered study, he went back to her. He sprinkled a magical mixture into the air about her, and he sang to her, his voice cracking. Her head tilted. The ritual was to no avail.

Three hundred more plus thirty-three days and thirty-three seconds, and he returned again hence. He adjusted the ratios of the mixture and added a lock of his own singed hair. He sang the song in a different key and altered the pronunciation of every fifteenth word.

She came to him then, pushing at and tearing through some manner of invisible membrane that screamed when breached and reddened the ground where it fell in shimmering tatters. He swept her up in his arms and brought her to his home. There, whilst she sat waiting on the drawing room settee, he lit the stove in the spare room, and he dusted and cleaned the room, presenting to her a comfortable bed, a writing desk, and a bell that might summon a servant bearing food or drink or whatever she wished. Before long, new shadows appeared on her face where eyes, nose, and mouth should be. When Features first saw this, he rubbed a specially made balm on his lips and kissed those shadows with chaste tenderness.

She came into his room one night and spoke for the first time, woke him from a deep, deathlike sleep. He thrashed and scrambled and pushed himself away until he saw that she meant him no harm. She loomed over him, her mouth still small and new, her teeth not much larger than grains of salt. He reached up and touched her face. Her head snapped back with a crack like a breaking branch and fell backward over her shoulders like the doffed hood of a cloak, her neck jutting upward like a bruised mountain. He sat up. With both hands he reached around as to embrace her and lifted her head back into place. Her face betrayed no pain, just a kind of bemused puzzlement. He whispered a healing spell, and her cervical vertebrae knitted itself back together with a sound like crackling fire.

Over the next several months, he watched her as she became herself. She spoke and read, but she did not speak of her past, and Features did not ask. Together they read from the dark book. Together they drank from secret springs. Together they washed in the blood of the innocent slain. Together they interrogated the moon and scooped its reflection in their cupped hands to sup at it. Together they grew fangs and bit at each other's flesh.

One day, they were sitting companionably by the pond in Child's Park after having meditated, basking in the air of glorious indefinite indolence, when a man approached them. His eyes were bruised, his lips and the flesh around his mouth mangled, dangling in dripping strips. They bade him sit. They found him of malleable mind and lost spirit, so they took him in and fed him. And taught him. On occasion he endeavored to abscond with jewels and gems and coins, and the cat always retrieved him. Their spirits never flagged. They never gave up hope. And one day, he led them back to his house in the woods. It was stocked through with books but had no running water, no room identifiable as a kitchen, no apparent bathroom.

Teach me, he had said to Features and his companion.

And so they taught him.

The tale continues as Grim Features and his paramour meet and take in a rogue's gallery of ne'er-do-wells, miscreants, and marginal folk and uncover the occult powers within each of them. The story turns when they encounter in an upper room of an abandoned house a man named Goodwin Leland.

The house stood in the center of the forest. The first-floor windows gaped open, screaming mouths with multitudinous translucent fangs of glass. The roof sagged like a damp sheet. Shutters lay like scratched-off scabs by the foundation, peeled paint like discarded skin dotted the dirt. Cormorants barked. A nearby brook bubbled like a feverish toddler's babble. We approached from the east, eager to explore the darkened interior. The ground floor had been cleared of any furnishings and decorations. A cluster of wire hangers lay entangled on the floor of the sole closet. On the unswept floor lay grit, dirt, and the occasional penny. The refrigerator door concealed only something dried and desiccated. The dingy walls bore slightly less dingy rectangles where pictures had hung.

The stairs creaked pitiably, decrying our invasive ascent. At the landing, a small round table stood on a small round rug as though afraid of stepping off it. On the table sat a phone without its handset, a cradle bereft of its occupant. We were startled to find that the upstairs looked to be that of a home in which people currently lived. All was clean and well kept, awash in sunlight to which the downstairs rooms seemed immune. An oriental runner, unfaded, mainly bright red, spanned the long hall. A wall clock ticked amiably. The odor of a freshly lit pipe wafted from somewhere along with the list of some flute-heavy classical music. We followed that trail to a small neat bedroom lined with teeming bookshelves and decorated with frilled curtains and broad paintings of verdant landscapes traversed by blur-faced, frolicking children. On the bed, facing away from us, sat a man cross-legged, the pipe jutting off leftward. Longish blonde hair framed a pinkish bald spot. He was staring at the dresser, upon which sat a glass container. And inside swam a small faceless human figure dressed in doll clothes. Its hairless face bore only a tiny red puncture wound where a mouth would sit. It butted its head against the glass soundlessly. At the bottom of this container lay another similar figure, dead on a floor of green emeralds.

The man sighed and spun himself around, making a mess of the bedspread in the process, spilling and then slapping at the contents of his pipe. His brown hair was heavily greased and severely parted on the left, like that of a boy whose mother insisted he look nice for church . . . though the mad look in his eye suggested an extremely non-traditional church indeed. Greasy wings of hair fanned out over his wax-caked ears. His waxed mustache reached out toward the walls. Though his clothes were neat and his face—except the ears—scrubbed and shaved, a reek of body odor and corruption emanated from him. "I've been expecting you," he said in a high, thin voice.

In the container, the humanoid thing began to hum—a staticky, rasping drone. The man on the bed gestured toward it. "I must introduce you to my great friend," he said. "He's doing tremendous things in radio these days."

Geist was also put off by conventional black magic: puerile desecrations, the spilling of semen, perversions of the Eucharist. Akin to children in a far corner of a playground, sniping and complaining, ridiculing the teacher instead of dragging the teacher to the lake in the woods and showing them the devil's hindquarters, face to distended face, and returning the teacher mad and raving to their classroom to pull the blinds, lock the door, and spread the dark word.

Geist did not seek proximity to the divine, except maybe for the purposes of sticking a knife in its side and twisting. Proximity to fear, *merging* with fear, *becoming* fear . . . *there* was a direct line to the true self.

So in those years, Geist read. The culmination of his reading led to the study of treatises on death. The fact of death had always been with him but somewhere in the background, behind his shadow, sliding through a synapse entwined with an impulse or a stray thought. He had seen it defied, but the revenants were tortured half-things, stuck in a wretched abyss between life and death. Their souls still rotted though their consciousness lived on. Now death loomed large, a great blot that prevented the fullness of his vision, a deep blur at the horizon like the strange, glowing colors that remained in your vision after staring too long at a strong light . . . except this would not go away. And so Geist read of resurrections, of reversals of death, of the most forbidden of magicks—the unthinkable reversal of death's last word.

In all the pages in all the forbidden books, he could find nothing about full corporeal resurrection, but after a time, he began to note elliptical passages in many of the tomes, some in other languages, dead languages. He began to compile them in his daybook. After years of this, he had most of what he needed, at least in the way of a plan. There was no hope of indefinitely prolonging life, but after the body had gone entirely to dust, save a swath of skin preserved and kept by a compatriot, there was a way to come back. Damaged, perhaps. Mad? Almost certainly. But back . . . to continue his work in dreams and to touch and feel and smell and taste.

And learning the totems and powders and baubles he would need to ensure his continuation (after such an abysmal interruption for which there would be no way around), he knew that he would have to travel, to barter and trade and purchase and, if necessary—and he knew it would indeed be necessary—to steal. Once the necessary items were in hand, they must be scattered so that his enemies might not thwart the scheme. Into the edifices of the unknowing and the innocent, to be brought to a public house on the appointed date. But first he had to acquire the items. He could not send emissaries, though he might wish to. No, he would have to be there.

Eldritch tomes in mobile homes
Mottled bones and toblerones

—Abrecan Geist, *Two-Line Poems*

Walter was full—"to the gills," as his father used to say—and dizzy but not unpleasantly so. It felt like sweet soda water buoying his spirit. He felt *free*. The man had talked all through the luncheon, the two alone at their own table, everything else a background blur, his monologue unspooling even as he gnawed on chicken bones and pulled gristle from between his teeth, even as he emptied bottle after bottle. He'd told Walter of a fat, blind God, sadistic and touchy and cruel, a killer of millions with a gore-strewn beard. He'd told of a devil who wanted people to be happy, to be free from the empty threat of punishment, to make full use of their bodies and brains. There was no heaven up above the clouds—this Walter had already suspected—and no hell! To think of it! Walter had always held in the back of his mind a certain skepticism about the promise of heaven, of eternal life, but he had pushed it back out of fear that God would send his spectral fingers into the meat of Walter's brain and pull out and expose his doubt like a ragged splinter, that with his secret sin having thus been found out, his place would be reserved in the center of hell's fiery lake, his skin eternally melting, his eyes boiling in their sockets, his skin charring and flaking. His fear of damnation was now supplanted by the specter of eternal nonexistence, but the man, who had introduced himself as Uncle Andrew (and requested that Walter address him as Uncle), had at one point leaned forward toward Walter and in a conspiratorial tone said, "But we will work on mortality, you and I, won't we."

The priest, who had been making the postprandial rounds, arrived at their table. "Gentlemen," he said. "I'm Father Perceval. It's a pleasure to see you here today. Young man. And good sir . . . sir, I don't recall seeing you at the service."

And Uncle Andrew's face . . . *changed*. His cheekbones rose and jutted, and a nest of parentheses appeared on either side of his mouth. His blue eyes glinted with red, and his canine teeth elongated just slightly. "*Father*," he said, his open mouth revealing a strangely sharpened tongue—the word in his mouth was as an unspeakable obscenity. The priest's face didn't register any offense. "A little bird told me that dessert is just around the corner," he said, and it occurred to Walter that Uncle Andrew might just want to devour the priest himself for his post-meal repast.

Walter's mom wandered out from a knot of ladies, laughing raucously, and dropped down in the seat next to him. The priest took the opportunity to sit at her other side; his voice went lower, and the two conferred like spies. Uncle Andrew raised an eyebrow at Walter, and the latter circled the table to sit at the bearded man's side.

Moments later, after having consumed a quantity of coffee and two towering, substantial wedges of cake—contrasted by a thin slice for Walter—the man leaned forward and looked at him warmly. Walter experienced a surge of filial emotion and wanted to listen to this man, to learn about the world from him. Even just the smell of his aftershave, pungent and stinking of alcohol, stirred something powerful in Walter.

"Now," Andrew said, "I will demonstrate for you a strange and dangerous power. I suspect you will be safe, but you may need this." He pulled from his vest pocket a flick knife with the evocative word *Châtellerault* etched on its side.

Walter glanced at his mother who was still deep in conversation with the priest. He held the knife at his side.

Uncle Andrew slumped in his seat, crossed his arms over his substantial belly, and closed his eyes. A moment later, he began to snore lightly. Then everything got strange.

Bill Valerio held his hands under his shirt against his swelling stomach. He had eaten far too much. Specifically, a stack of pancakes, a triple bacon cheeseburger with fries, a hillock of scrambled eggs, all topped off with two slices of chocolate cake still chilly in the middle from its prolonged confinement in the diner's freezer. He had also consumed no less than four full glasses of ice water, ice and all. Compounding the feeling of nearly panicked discomfort was the fact that she was out there in the parking lot. The jogger. He knew she was out there without even having to look. Further, he knew that her bent-backwards neck had stretched out to a terrible length like that Stretch Armstrong doll he'd had as a kid, the one whose limbs and neck could be pulled until they were five times their original length and thin as pencil-lead. Her head was now down at the back of her knees, staring up into the restaurant window. Her elasticized skin had ruptured in several places along the length of the neck, exposing bone encased in powerful, rancid-smelling pinkish gelatin. He knew this without having to look, just as he knew that one touch of the oozing gel would burn his skin away as surely and as devastatingly as a touch of lava.

A cackle came from somewhere behind him and he jumped, nearly knocking over his glass. He got up and made his unsteady way to the bathroom, assiduously avoiding looking out the window. He was going to be sick. It would be bad.

1965. As the biplane dropped below the cloud level, Walter Clough, a man of twenty years (twenty and a half) with a wispy mustache, slicked-back dark hair, and a lopsided grin, kept a slightly inebriated eye on Geist as the latter gazed out upon the towers and spires and onion-shaped domes topped with small gold orbs, upon the teeming dusty streets and the jostling motorcars. Geist's eyes were clouded, his forehead creased with tension. He did not care for flying, and the sputtering, uneven sound of the engines coupled with the turbulent bouncing of the aircraft sat quite poorly with him. He had confessed to having not slept well the previous few nights, worried at the prospect of being rooked or swindled, given a useless bag of dust in return for the considerable sum he was prepared to pay, not to mention the cost and the complex logistics of arranging the flight.

Walter endeavored to cheer him. "This is the land of caliphs and djinns, of viziers and dervishes," he called out. "If our pilot isn't watchful, at any moment, we might crash into the side of Mount Qaf or pull into our engines a hapless gent on a flying carpet."

"You're thinking of Persia," Geist muttered, wrenching his mouth briefly into an accommodating half smile. He adjusted his cane, worrying at it with his fingers, and glowered once again out the window. He was a dark magus, cloistered with his cats and his books and his secrets; he was a man who romped in the deep woods with devils and strange beasts, a thaumaturgist who trafficked in strange powders and dangerous grimoires. So that he was susceptible to airsickness was a shock to Walter. Impressively though, Walter made a point of noting, the old man did not regurgitate.

The heat wilted everything, made all seem slowed-down and just slightly blurred. The old man and the young man stood side by side, jet-lagged and damp, stretching their limbs and groaning at the curb. Geist appeared to be grateful to be again on solid ground, perhaps a spot of anxiety remaining due to the alien aspects of this ancient country as well as prematurely dreading the return flight. A green, profusely dented Hindustan Ambassador pulled up, puffing little clouds of white from its hindquarters. The driver grinned a mishmash of bright white teeth through the open window, dark spectacles obscuring his eyes, a thin mustache lining his upper lip. He exited the car with a somehow cheerful grunt, a smallish man sharply dressed in a Nehru jacket and pressed slacks, and embraced Clough and Geist, the latter distinctly discomfited by the gesture. With a thin-fingered hand at the end of a spindly arm, the man opened the door and bade the visitors enter into the back seat. Sweat poured off the trio as they bounced over rutted roads, looking out at stacked blocks of apartment porches, at markets topped with awnings marked in that beautiful yet—to us untutored westerners—impenetrable lettering, at cars and motorcycles and people carrying long bundles of bamboo on their shoulders, at people shouting, gesticulating in small, intense groups. The air smelled of bodies, of sweat and food and garbage and car exhaust.

The Dark Swami, a bald, white-bearded old bird with youthful eyes that betrayed bemused impatience, sat cross-legged on an expansive pillow adorned with stitched images of great birds with worms dangling from their beaks, the gold fringe that framed it swaying slightly in the spiced air. Spider-like chandeliers dangled lamps of cut glass, glowing gold—and below, elaborate, erotic frescoes and tapestries and framed portraits of fanged and elaborately costumed rakshasas with wild eyes. Tall, wood-backed chairs ringed the room. Groups of low-slung settees and more gold-fringed pillows adorned its center among many-fingered ferns, thulasi plants, stone plinths bearing strange idols, and elaborate statuary, depicting grinning men locked in embraces erotic or violent—it was difficult to determine.

Geist dug into his vest pocket and pulled from it a pink glass phial. He held it up before the shaman. "Leeds air," he said, "captured high atop Mount Nonotuck." From his other pocket, he extracted a wad of bills.

The swami snatched the phial from Geist's hand and held it to his ear, squeezing shut his eyes and holding a finger up to his mouth to forestall speech or noise. Everyone quieted. Eyes smiling, he formed his hand into the universal OK gesture and set the phial down atop a crumbling plinth. "Now," he said in heavily accented English, "the word may be heard in our great country." A bloated hijrah separated himself from the shadows of an alcove and came forth with a glass dome, held in gloved hands. He placed the dome atop the plinth and hastened back into the shadows with the treasure. Only then did the swami take the money, without ceremony, and tuck it into the sleeve of his robe.

The swami raised one eyebrow and then the other, grinning like a butterflied fish. He stood. With his long, gnarled fingernail, he flicked a small bell that sat on a tall table. Two diapered hijrahs pulled back curtains that lined a section of the western wall and held them at their bulging bellies as from the dark doorway stepped ten women in sashes of silk. They lined up before Geist whose eyes widened. He wiped at his mouth. The women's expressions were blank, their feet bare. Geist sniffed the air to find wafts of flower and fruit and secret flesh. "This is how you like them, yes?" the swami said in a buttery baritone. "Contoured and tall? Callipygian and heavy of breast? Long, straight hair?"

Geist moistened his lips with his tongue and said something in a low voice. Walter could not make it out.

The women spun themselves from their scarves in a slinking dance, and as they set about Geist, his expression softened. For the nonce, he would be troubled by neither worry nor woe.

Later, as he reposed in a grand tub fashioned after a conch shell, regretfully scrubbing from his body their kisses and caresses, their sweetness and their filth, he contemplated the next leg of travel to the country of China. He feared air travel and longed desperately for home.

He resolved to put those thoughts aside for now. He let himself sink in the warm water up to his chin. He pushed back his hair and gazed up at the intricately wrought tin ceiling as the water lapped around the island of his belly. For a time, he looked for shapes in the patterns, imagining it as an inverted city of mazes and corridors, causeways and sunken walks. Then he closed his eyes and let the undiscovered colors of his mind expand the city into something neon and gaudy. He sank slightly in the tub, the smell of incense making him quite sleepy.

The next day, after a deep and lush sleep, the two men rose to find the swami and the women absent. Their luggage had been placed by the door. On top of Geist's suitcase sat a leather envelope. Walter opened it to find six waxy bags of powders, folded and stapled shut. He held it up for Geist to inspect.

"These will do," Geist said. "These will do quite well."

The guests slowed in their movements until they were as painted figures in a medieval fresco. The sky darkened, its surface rippling and going dark green, as though it was held up by a sheet of translucent industrial cellophane. Clouds scudded by just beyond the surface like a school of malformed fish in a dishwater river. Distant thunder stuttered and chuckled, and a great wind lashed at the treetops. The cloths rose from the tables and fluttered just above the guests' heads like restless ghosts. Walter fled to the gift table and ducked down, peeking over the top.

As he watched in terror, a hollow-cheeked man in papal vestments emerged from the darkness of the woods, floating, his bare, blistered arms stretched out like those of Christ on the cross, palms up. A three-tiered crown adorned his head, bejeweled with sparkling diamonds, lapis lazuli, cuprite, and olivine, scattered like glowing crumbs along meandering trails of steel spikes and grommets. Around each ridge that separated the tiers, miniature chariots sped, led by snorting horses. Small doors opened and closed in the surface of the ornate hat, revealing yellow eyes and tiny clawed hands like those of hairless mice. He surveyed the frozen crowd, smiling eyes gleaming over a sharp, downturned nose. A fanged grin split his face, the chin below it pointing as though to select a victim. The gossamer scarf that crossed his chest was decorated with depictions of occult emblems, broken keys, bent crosses, and teeth.

Behind the man, the trees uprooted themselves soundlessly, rose a few feet, roots dangling like tentacles, and began to spin. Faster and faster they went, shedding their leaves and then their branches. Eventually, entire limbs went with great cracking sounds, shooting up into the sky until they were distant, fragmented lines. The trees, now bare poles with patches of bark, slowly tipped until they were horizontal. They bent into slender oscillating patterns like soundwaves.

The mother held aloft her newly baptized baby. Ecstatic joy stretched open her mouth and eyes until the skin around them cracked open into red clefts. The infant tittered and fussed, eyes squinting, tiny red fists punching at the air, little feet cycling. Through the air, the unholy pope swam until he hovered above mother and child. He brought his thin-fingered hands to his chest, palms up, creating a skeletal bassinet. Moisture beaded on the infant's head and flew into the pope's waiting palms. He clenched them, drawing back his lips to reveal his teeth, and his eyes glowed a sickly gold. Then he opened his palms once again and nodded his head.

The mother gingerly placed the child into the pope's palms and knelt in supplication. From the sky descended a coterie of angels. Sickly thin, cadaverous gray things with wilted wings and gape-mouths, they knelt in a tight circle around the pope and fought to kiss his feet, snarling, snapping and hissing at one another, drawing blood, gore-tipped feathers dropping to the ground. The grass beneath the dark pope went brown, wilted, and began to sink into the earth, leaving a circle of black soil. The angels backed up in a panic from the widening hole, some still snarling, others whining like dogs. Swirling eddies formed, the dirt clouding into the air. Pope and infant sank into the earth. The mother crawled over to the hole—it was so deep, endlessly deep—and dove in. The guests began to emerge from their stasis, looking around them, trying, it seemed to Walter, to make sense of this new strangeness, to shake off the murk of their induced coma. As a chorus, they all cried out, and that's when the angels attacked.

Two of them fell upon a limping elderly woman, who had turned to flee, and slammed her to the ground. Her breath came in great whoops as they began to stab her with their claws—she couldn't muster enough air even to scream. A younger woman ran over and tried to pull the things off but yanked her hands away. They were smoking and red. She bolted across the yard and plunged them into one of the ice buckets. Another angel loped up behind her and pushed her head into the bucket, held it under, batting away her flailing arms and cackling like a demented infant. All across the lawn, men and women battled the angels to little avail. Soon, bloody bodies lay scattered and defiled. One angel came scrambling toward Walter, streamers of gelatinous drool swaying from its black lips. It leapt to the top of the table. Walter hit the button on the knife. The blade swung out. Walter planted it in the center of the angel's foot. It howled and crumpled. With a muffled pop, its gray-fleshed ankle snapped. Its jaw hit the table hard on its way down, yellow teeth flying into the air.

Uncle Andrew was suddenly there, standing on the ground into which the evil pope had sunk. He was laughing and applauding. The angels fizzled and disappeared. The few partygoers still alive huddled behind tipped-over tables or else fled across the razed landscape that used to be the woods. "Let's go retrieve your mother," Andrew said, taking Walter's hand in his. Walter looked up at him.

"Yes, she survived. She's passed out in an upstairs bedroom. We'll wake her up and go get some ice cream. What do you say?" They walked across the bloodstained grass to the house. Inside, carpeted stairs rose to a second-floor landing at their left alongside a hall leading back to the kitchen; to their right was a dining room with an expansive table and glass corner cabinets. Andrew held up a hand, indicating Walter should wait, when the priest appeared on the landing above. His hair was standing up in points, his belt and collar undone, his face pink. He called out, "You filthy devil!" Then he raised a pistol in a trembling hand and fired. The shot hit the banister by Uncle Andrew's hand, splintering it. The priest muttered and spun the chamber, started down the stairs. Andrew raised his hands in the air. They shook rapidly, blurring until his fingers appeared to lose their shape, becoming elastic. His eyes rolled back in his head, and he began to recite something in a strange language. He backed away through the front door, down the porch, onto the front lawn, still chanting, Walter keeping pace just behind, making sure Andrew was between him and the gun-toting priest who followed, fussing with the gun.

"Fall to the ground," Andrew shouted, and the priest's eyes went wide as his legs slid backward, out from under him, and he landed hard on his stomach.

"Take your true form," Andrew called, and the priest's bones went to jelly, and he oozed into the grass, dropping the pistol. He stretched himself long and thin. Arms at his sides, fingers held straight out and tightly together, he slithered like a snake along the ground, eyes rolled back so far that they were just whites under a lightning-like lattice of red veins. His mouth stretched back almost to his ears and opened to reveal two fangs like scythes of ivory. From between them, his long, forked tongue flickered.

Walter bolted as the snake approached, and he ran into the open garage and saw exactly what he needed: a steel-bladed, round-point shovel. He grabbed it and ran back, tossed it to Andrew, who caught it one handed, grabbing it at its midpoint with both hands, and stabbed it down into the snake-priest's neck. It emitted a strange, gargling chortle, and Andrew stabbed down again and again until the head separated from the body. Blood shot onto the lawn in jets from the head and from the body. "Keep an eye on it," said Uncle Andrew as he handed Walter the shovel and went back into the house. A few minutes later, the three were on the Interstate in Andrew's old Ford, heading into their respective futures—Walter riding shotgun, his mother passed out in the back seat. Sirens called out somewhere behind them, the faint, distant, mournful wails of birds arriving too late to catch the worm.

The frenzied, hallucinatory nightmare that had overtaken the Look Diner abated, just like that. The structure and the decor unchanged. Normalcy regained. Waiters ran to-and-fro, some with order pads, some with trays of steaming food and drinks. A couple at the register signed their receipt and wrote in the tip. Forks scraped plates. Busboys cleared tables, wiped them down. The dazed and

destabilized denizens of the diner stared all about them, wondering if maybe there was something in the water, if they'd been dosed there or somewhere else as they went about their day. People rubbed their temples, blinked, wetted their lips.

Walter looked at Carla. The old man would love her, he thought, will love her—her dark aesthetic, all black and silver and shining red, her cruel lips and bright, intelligent, curious green eyes. His gaze swept over to Leeza. With her blonde hair tied atop her head and her coolly assessing yet capricious gaze, she resembled nothing so much as the tawdry, careless queen of some neglected gimcrack country. He put a patronly hand on the back of her neck, and with his other hand, he gripped Carla's knee in a somewhat more carnal manner. "Are you ready, ladies?" he asked. They nodded and in small voices answered in the affirmative. He gripped the arms of his chair and rose. Carla handed him his cane. With surprising agility, he touched its tip to the tabletop and leapt up almost to the ceiling, landing in the table's center, his legs together, arms outstretched. He flipped the cane. It spun in the air, a blurred brown circle, and he caught it head-down. He swept from the table the bone-strewn plates, the crumpled, stained napkins, the glasses of melting ice, the coffee mugs. Everyone turned to face him. The white-haired cook came out from the kitchen, his knife gripped in his right hand. From behind the glass-topped half wall that separated the kitchen from the dining room, he watched.

"Ladies," Walter said, "and gentlemen. And everyone in-between and outside. I want to welcome you to the show of which you didn't know, the obsecration, the resurrection, the dream you weren't aware you'd all been waiting for. Some of you will play a part. Others will bear witness. After, none of you will be the same." He considered. "Well, no one will."

The ladies stood, kicked aside their chairs. One by one, he helped them up onto the table, their ascent slightly clumsier than his had been. "I see that we have your attention," he said. "Shall we begin the ceremony?"

The Resurrection of Abrecan Geist

Those blue and violet orbs, oblong or squashed, from when you've looked too long at a light, the ones that float in the foreground of your vision, are coming to life, growing teeth.

—Abrecan Geist, *Encyclopedia of Dreams*

CHRISTIANITY IS AN ANALOGUE OF THE POLITICAL PARTY THAT ACCUSES *its opponent of its own crimes. God embodies all the qualities worshippers attribute to the devil. He is the Adversary. He is the Father of Lies. The deceiver. The enemy. Let us not mince words: the manufacturer and distributor of flies is by definition the lord of same. His throne is of gore-streaked bone, his miter and his teeth stained permanently red, his gullet choked with the innards of the innocent. He subsists on the cake of suffering, and fealty is the frosting. He demands abstinence and abjection and peddles in return the false hope of some far-too-white halcyon eternity with tennis courts and cucumber sandwiches and treacly music piped in.*

Not for me.

Not for any thinking person. And most certainly not for anyone whose lust is not for the antiseptic and the anodyne. Instead, for a life lived fervently, fiercely, savagely. I became an apostate the moment I heard Geist's voice. I cast my lot in with the devil and have never looked back except to mark the trajectory of the bottle bomb I hurled upon my departure. I am not a follower of Abrecan Geist and not an apostle. I am the man's friend, his comrade, and his protector. He started out as a father figure to me, and one day, I will in turn be there at his second birth. I will in a very real way be both a father and a midwife and again a friend to my beloved fallen angel.

—Walter Clough, *Clough Stuff,*
the Musings of Walter Clough, Vol. 3
(from Chapter 8: That Poor Bastard on the Cross)

You've been listening to WXXT. That was a dandy little finger-snapper by the inimitable Wally "Too-Tough" Clough. Before that, we heard Paula and the Pustules with "Taste My Tumor." The time is 11:13 p.m. Or 2:30 a.m. Or 6:16 a.m. Who can say? It's a hot one and getting hotter. Clouds pile one atop the other, a billowing, burgeoning tower of turbulent black hate, tinged with cottony mucor and illuminated from within by flickering flashes of lightning, rising into the great, silent mystery, the unknowable infinity that surrounds the earth and reaches beyond our ability to imagine.

I don't know about you, listeners, but I've been dreaming a lot lately. It seems to me that whenever I shut my eyes, the world goes . . . *funny.* A dog walking on its hind legs lurches from a shadowed alleyway, a proliferation of wizened human hands reaching from its stretched-out mouth. Pastries grow legs and stingers and razor-sharp teeth, and they leap to the throats of the old men who huddle at the counter over steaming cups of something science-fiction green. Armless men dance with abandon on rooftops, winged leeches swollen to the size of cantaloupes clinging to the crowns of their heads. Children climb the church steeples like spiders and shit acidic webs onto the parishioners and priests as they flee. The dead sing obscene hymns from under their gravestones, sweet, sickly harmonies that blacken the grasses and dissolve the wings of butterflies.

But enough about me and enough, for now, about dreams—we're going live now to the Look Diner where we await the triumphant return of our resident mystic, our abstruse muse of the news, Abrecan Geist. Our street team will be on hand in the parking lot with promotional T-shirts, coffee mugs, and cremation urns. Tell 'em old Ben Stockton sent you, and you'll get a little something for it. Something insidious and aggressive. Something that no antibiotic nor emollient can dispel. But look at me, rambling on. Let's go live to the Look.

Marci and Shantaya stand out back by the fenced-in dumpster. The resident peepers sing their nightly chorus, unchanging, untiring, punctuated by the occasional buzz of the blue bug zappers screwed into the fence posts. Everything glows a sickly orange under the lot lights. Marci pulls a pack of American Spirits from her apron pocket, shakes out one for herself and a second for Shantaya, who lights both with a purple Bic. "Christ, it stinks out here," Marci says. She puts the cigarette in her mouth and smacks her forearm, smearing a dead mosquito onto her apron with a grimace.

"That's why they make us smoke out here instead of in front. They want us to stop. *They care about our health.*"

Marci snickers. The two smoke in uneasy silence. An airplane screams somewhere high up in the firmament, its red lights blinking, winking, and they turn their faces upward and watch as it penetrates the burgeoning citadel of clouds. The lights go a strange orange and disappear. "Weird night," Shantaya says, not knowing exactly what she means by it other than a general misgiving. Something is wrong. Or *going to be* wrong.

"Wicked."

"You know what I mean?"

"Yeah. Hard to put it in words. I shoulda called in sick. Darren and Rob are going down to Hartford to see a ball game. Yard Goats against the Fisher Cats. Rather be there than here."

She takes a drag from her cigarette, exhales a blue cloud that rises until it is subsumed by the great black sky. "Rather be anywhere."

As if in reply, a muted rustling sounds from somewhere inside the dumpster— and then a loud metallic thump like something trying to get their attention from inside. The women laugh nervously as they stomp out their cigarettes in a hurried dance, which looks almost choreographed, and hustle back inside. As they reach the dining room from the darkened banquet facility, Marci grabs Shantaya's arm and squeezes. Hard. A man is standing on one of the tables, and the two strippers that'd come in with him are rearranging the chairs.

"What the *fuck*?" Marci says.

Well, that was unexpectedly good. I don't know about you, but I most certainly overdid it. The steak was so tender and bloody and blue though. Look at me. I'm an unholy mess. My shirt is done for. Soaked right through. My skin too, the bloody grease penetrating layers of dermis, discoloring them, breaking down my cells, surging toward my veins. Going to have to throw my skin out too, I guess. I'll just step out of it like a rubber suit and put the whole sopping mess into one of those leak-proof containers with the biomedical hazard symbol, the one that looks like three circles of deadly pincers.

I'm a happy man when I have a full stomach. When fat and gristle crowd my teeth. Whenever I am, for any reason, covered in blood. It's the lifeforce, you know, blood, and it's such a treat to see it right out there in the open like a dark secret finally exposed to the light. I suspect we'll see more of it before this night is over. Maybe mine. Maybe yours. It's sticky and a bitch to wash off, but I just love the stuff. It's like wine squeezed from human grapes.

There's been a lull. Have you noticed? Everything is strangely, surreally . . . *normal*. You'd almost think you and I were sitting in a normal diner on an average night. The only thing odd is the way some of the diners are looking out the window. They look fearful. Maybe it's the moon. It looks like the chipped and stained tusk of some great celestial mastodon. Like me, it's showing its age. But don't be fooled. To a point, age does not signal a loss of power. Quite the opposite in fact.

Case in point: check out the old man with the white beard. It appears that he's gearing up for a speech.

"There it is," said Walter, pointing. Geist lowered his head and looked out the smudged cab window to see a shabby building, stained and crumbling, nestled between two tenements as though for warmth. The cab slid to the curb. While Walter paid the fare, Geist clambered out onto the sidewalk and stretched his limbs. Too much travel. He was ready for home.

Bao Xie peered out the window at the two men exiting a car on the street below. They were as out of place as hippopotamuses at a horse farm. The bearded one wore a suit a size too small, the necktie too short. The other wore a hat and monocle and exuded an air of menace and dark royalty. Bao had spent the afternoon reconciling accounts, puzzling out and resolving discrepancies, in a work-trance as hours slipped by him unnoticed like spies. Now he stood by a button on the wall and waited for the buzzer to sound.

As it sounded and Bao hit the door release, Chao walked in and lit the two candles at the outer corners of Bao's desk. At Bao's nod, he unlocked the desk drawer and pulled out the satchel. Bao put his arms behind his back. Moments later, the knock came at the door, and Chao bade the two men enter.

"Gentlemen," Bao said, "shall we do business?"

"Perhaps a brief introduction first?" the bearded one said, sounding vaguely affronted. He introduced himself as Walter Clough. "And you know of Mr. Geist." Geist frowned and nodded. Clough pulled from his vest pocket two small vials of muddy water. "Straight from the Mill River," he said.

Bao opened the satchel and gathered the rings. He held them out to Clough. Though they looked dull and marred, through their curious design and something ineffable, an aura of mystic power surrounded them like boiling air. Geist grinned a wolfish grin. Clough raised his eyebrows. "A point of clarification before you part with these," the latter said. "If these rings are so powerful, so valuable . . . why part with them?"

Bao nodded. The men must have seen it in his face. He was never adept at hiding his emotions. To part with these rings—their history, their hereditary significance—was unthinkable. And he was about to do the unthinkable.

He said:

My grandfather passed down these rings to me. He was on his deathbed in his sunlit room, in a sea of motes like tiny angels, facing the infinite, struck mute by the cancer that had devastated his throat. His attorney was there, mostly mute as well but by choice. The attorney dropped the satchel—this very satchel—on the bed between my grandfather's feet and pulled out the rings one by one. He then presented me with a sheaf of instructions so byzantine and voluminous that all I could feel was intimidation. Though the set was incomplete—a burglar had seen to that, absconding with two of the rings and several important grimoires—the attorney informed me that they still held tremendous power. I promised to study the rings, swore out loud to it. I saw peace spread like light across my grandfather's face. Peace and release. He could die now.

The attorney must have seen by my expression that I was overwhelmed. He spoke slowly and in simple terms. Depending upon which rings one wore, and upon which fingers one wore them, and upon which way they were turned, and at what velocity they were adjusted, and upon the formation in which one held one's fingers, one could alter the world to one's own specifications, bring wealth, acquire lovers, hold dominion over men. Meticulousness, accuracy to the millionth of the smallest measurement, was paramount.

At any rate, we sat in silence: the attorney lost in whatever litigious thoughts occupied his mind, me mulling over what he had told me, allowing myself the luxury of considering the results of the work without thinking of the actual work. We watched over the old man. Two hours later, he gasped, tensed up, and seemed to sink slightly into the bed. It was over.

That night, I leafed through the instructions in my one-room apartment. They were anything but straightforward. They contained contradictions, vague language, ambiguous phrasings, illustrations that did not conform to the anatomy of the human hand as concerned the number of joints in the fingers, not to mention the number of fingers. There were passages in what seemed to be another language whose characters were foreign to me, unrecognizable as any human language. I could not reasonably append my scholarly work, not to mention my social life, with study of this dense and jumbled occult manuscript. I'd fail out of school with nothing to show for it.

So it was that two years later, having failed out of college even without the secondary burden of occult study, having secured part-time work in a food market, barely covering my portion of the shared rent, in my lowest moment, that I fished the instructions from my trunk and began to subject them to serious study. I filled the hours of my empty days, honed my ability to concentrate. Within four months, I could cause small objects to tremble; inside of eight months I could hasten (or decelerate if I so wished) the growth of vegetables, shrubbery, grass, and small trees. Flipping to the later passages, I saw that with the proper discipline, I could free myself from a life of servitude, of commuting to work, of sweating awake at night, anxiety spinning like a dervish in my gut.

And then a new neighbor moved in upstairs. Li Wei was an exceedingly odd fellow. The first time I saw him, he was standing on the walk in front of the apartment house, staring gape-eyed and gape-mouthed at the sky as though frozen in some kind of rapture. He looked down at me dismissively and walked away shaking his head as though it was I who was acting strangely. Later that afternoon, he introduced himself. I was leaving my apartment, and when I opened my door, he was standing in the hall facing said door, too far away from it to knock. "How long have you been standing here?" I asked, and instead of answering, he said his name and nodded. He informed me that he would be moving into his apartment the next day.

He wore oversized, brightly spangled jackets. He often went barefoot on the filthy streets. He appeared to regularly shave off his eyebrows. Bracketing his mouth were patches of mustache hair while above his lip the skin was as bare as that upon his brow.

I'd assumed that the ensuing noise and clamor was just the sound of someone moving in, arranging furniture, getting settled. But it went on for weeks, day and night. Thumping, scraping, stomping. Whistling. Did this man work? Was he ever not home? And then there were his guests. Men and women of all nationalities, it sounded like. I heard the babbling sounds of English, of percussive German, slurred French. Again, at all hours, at times the voices raised in anger, at times in what sounded like religious or sexual ecstasy. Insomnia became normality.

Furious one night, nearly insane and on the verge of hallucinating, I went upstairs and banged on the man's door, cursing, ranting. Lights sprung from under the other doors in the hallway like curious ghosts. The door swung open, revealing a sparsely decorated living room, a sagging couch, a tapestry depicting an obscene orgy, and a three-legged table with only a lit cigarette on its surface. My neighbor was naked.

I forgot I was wearing one of the rings. As I unleashed my fury at Li Wei, I unconsciously twisted the ring. The lights in the apartment brightened until they were nearly blinding, and then they popped one after another like fireworks. Li Wei backed up, looking all around him. His eyes widened. He covered his ears. Then he went to his knees and vomited a viscous orange string onto his sleeveless shirt, where it clung like a centipede. "Make it stop," he said in a pathetic whimper.

I removed the ring from my finger. "Now, keep quiet," I said, "or move away. I'm done with you."

Li curled up on the floor. He looked up at the ring I held between my thumb and forefinger and then raised his gaze to meet mine. His ugly grimace morphed into an uglier grin.

It was three days later that I arrived home to find my apartment had been ransacked. Clothes lay strewn on the floor; the oven door hung open like a gasping mouth; my mattress lay askew on the frame, flayed open and gutted; the chair cushions had suffered a similar fate. The box (not hidden, I hasten to add—it sat in a prominent position on a small table in the living room) in which I kept the rings lay open, but all the rings were still there, arranged as they had been when

I'd last looked at them. However, closer inspection revealed they were gilded with a layer of brownish dust. I wiped it clear, disturbed. From the box, I pulled a ring I'd privately named the Dragon Tongue and slid it onto my index finger.

Gentlemen, you think you know pain. I thought I did. I never knew the pain I knew when that ring reached the base of my finger. It was hotter than the whitest fire, an ache like a hot blade, constriction like that of a thread pulled taut. I tried to pry the ring from my finger, and it was glued on, stuck fast. When I was able to pull it away, which took all the strength I had in me, the skin came with it. All of the skin, the nail, pulled from the bone like an inverted sock. And the pain I felt, the pain of a finger stripped clean? In contrast with the touch of the ring, it felt like relief.

And then Li Wei stood before me, his grin wide and vicious. "So much for your rings," he said. "You can never hurt me nor anyone with them again. And the best part, the juiciest part? I can. Anyone can. Anyone but you. Such is the nature of the spell I have cast."

With that, he walked over to the box that sat between us and reached for the rings. I pulled the pistol from my belt and shot him in the throat. It was the only act of violence I have ever committed, and I do not in the slightest regret it.

Standing at the griddle, Jabin, the white-coiffed man hewn of grease, spittle, and spindle, stares down a dozen bubbling, hissing Argus eyes of eggs, silver dollar pancakes just beyond them like a comic book character's thought bubbles. He feels other eyes on him too, human eyes, sizing him up, taking his measure.

A cook should always have the right knife for the job; that was how the saying used to go. But in most cases, a chef's knife will do whatever you need done. It will dice, julienne, mince, chop, and pierce. Do it neatly, do it right. As long as you keep it sharp, run it up and down the honing steel, back and forth, making a kind of skewed, moving cross. But Jabin wondered, will it stop an unholy resurrection deep in enemy territory—in devil-stained Leeds at the Look Diner?

No, for this Jabin needs *the* knife. Forged in a Roman catacomb older than Christ, blessed by a nephew of the Leper Priest of Belgium, moved by his leprologist to Prague, where in a high-end brothel in the penthouse of a building owned by a defrocked cardinal it had drained the lifeblood from the throat of Oalejr, a powerful minion of Mastema himself. The knife brought by boat to a port in New York City and transferred by a coterie of angels to Leeds and placed in the care of a group of low-level functionaries. But there was no way to retrieve that knife now. He will have to make do with the chef's knife. If only he could find peace with that.

Interlude. After many years of dormancy, the dreams returned. That damned ventriloquist dummy boring through his gray matter like a parasite. Terrible images and visions tormented him through his waking hours, superimposed over his daily rituals and routines. He could not even escape them in sleep, for dreams encroached on his unconsciousness almost nightly. That grinning maniac in a tuxedo gesturing with long, feminine fingers, performing a grotesque aria. Skating under a spotlight at a dark ice rink, a blue bloom of intestines protruding from its groin. Rising steaming and pink and wild-eyed from a pool of black and red lava. Flying across a gray-cloud sky, black wings flapping majestically, gloppy tendrils of drool swimming around its face like a mask of tentacles. Strolling through some teeming foreign bazaar, leading on a leash an emaciated, blood-soaked, boil-faced monkey that bared its fangs at the heedless throngs.

He was used to causing fear, not suffering from it.

One night, a thought—*I must have that dummy*—woke him from the latest dream: that hideous monkey with its vicious eyes and yellow fangs, blood caked in its eyelashes, the grinning dummy tugging impatiently on the leash. That day when the hour was reasonable, Geist telephoned the theater where he'd first seen the abomination perched menacingly on the lap of a tuxedo-clad ventriloquist. He had to encounter the thing that haunted him in the hope that seeing it again would sap it of its power. Surely it couldn't be that hideous. A weary-sounding woman answered. Geist asked her patience. Could she possibly locate the name of a ventriloquist who had performed as part of a vaudeville revue? He remembered the name of another performer—Spettrini—and the range of years in which the show may have occurred. He left his number. Then he sat, brooding, fists under his chin.

The woman called back four hours later and provided not only the name of the ventriloquist, Albert McCutcheon, stage name Andrew Valiente, but also his address, which she admitted might not be current. It was about two days away by train. The ventriloquist himself did not have a telephone. Geist considered writing the fellow a letter but decided a personal visit was in order, if only to exit the routine of his days, to take action immediately rather than wait for the vagaries and caprices of the postal service.

He liked to travel by train. It was an opportunity to clear his busy mind, to shake off the recent events. The day prior to the trip, he and Nicolas Lusk had been conducting a ritual to try to extract information from the freshly dead skull of Ellison Glumson III, the notorious shape-shifting shaman of Haydenville.

Glumson had been killed in a most inauspicious manner; he had been crossing King Street, distracted perhaps, and had been run down by a Ford roadster, knocked right out of his Oxfords, thrown over the hood of the car, bouncing off the roof, landing messily on the curb. Those who ran over to him reported an unnatural coldness emanating from the body. The roadster had drifted slowly to the curb, one tire flat, smoke pouring from its grille, the driver himself dead, inexplicably decapitated, his head resting in his lap, a serene look on his dying face, his lips moving slightly. A loud pop sounded, and Glumson's body burst into flames. A passerby endeavored to put out the flames with his greatcoat until some of the waitstaff from the nearby restaurant ran out with buckets of water to finish the job.

Lusk had later retrieved the skull, leaving behind him a dead coroner and a funeral home in flames. The skull was fresh, muscle and singed flesh clinging to parts of it, unkempt hair in patches, blue lips, a cracked white tongue like a dog turd on a sun-scorched sidewalk. The eyes had sunk in. Geist and Lusk had sat it on a folded tapestry, and Lusk rubbed goat's bane on the tongue as Geist read aloud the applicable text from the *Libellus Vox Larvae.* "Get it farther back on the tongue," Geist muttered, and Lusk did so, jabbing his finger around the soft palate. Minutes passed without incident.

"Speak!" Geist shouted, impatient. "Tell us how you rearrange yourself! Impart to us your secret!" Instead of replying, the mouth clacked, and a spittle-filled hiss sounded somewhere from inside. Fishy breath filled the room. The muscles slid across the face, and the skull cracked, the jaw elongating and jutting forward. The bones above the nose splintered, the empty eyes sliding closer together, and re-fused. "I didn't ask for a goddamned *demonstration,*" Geist sighed. The skull settled and whispered something incomprehensible. It was over.

Now, he watched the landscape pass before him: the backsides of city streets, trash-strewn courtyards with bent and twisted chain-link fences, rusted-out switching stations, the skeletons of greenhouses, disused parking lots. He let himself get lost in it, letting the previous day's failing fall away. Likewise, he pushed away the anxious anticipation of finally facing down the ventriloquist dummy that tormented his sleeping hours. He dozed, jotted notes in his journal, watched the other passengers, mused on matters great and small. The hours lurched by.

The squealing of the stopping train woke him. Outside the scratched-up window loomed the station, a long gray slumbering beast. Geist gathered his things and rose. Standing on the platform, he unfolded his map. A red X in the center of a tangle of streets. Geist walked, or rather lumbered, down streets lined with moribund businesses and boarded-up storefronts. A gray blanket of clouds lay overhead, as low as chimney smoke. Geist fancied that one could reach up and touch it from the top of the taller buildings. It would feel, he surmised, like cold cotton. He fancied also that the cloud never left this gloomy mill town whose factories lay dead like hardened worms and that gloom was its longest-running habitué, perhaps the very founder of the town. The slump-shouldered residents marked his presence with muted alarm, cleared him a path. They likely considered him a local luminary of some kind, a personage who surely had something to do with the machinations of the powerful, some great operator behind the scenes. Geist had that effect. Maybe they harbored a secret hope that he'd arrived to dispel the cloud and free the town from some ancient curse. More likely though, Geist's grim, severe countenance probably had them thinking he was there to do the cloud's dark business.

The house stood tall and gray and stately on a hillock overgrown with dead grass, a meandering iron fence tangled with curled dead branches hemming it in. Geist passed through the open gate, climbed the forty stairs to the over-large front door (which was painted bright red), and knocked. His heart thrummed in his chest.

The door swung open. Two ancient grinning Dobermans sat on the faded oriental runner, all red-rimmed eyes and sagging jowls, long pink tongues bouncing in synchrony. Geist backed up a step as one of them let loose a fusillade of hoarse barks, its companion looking on approvingly. "Theophrastus! Bombastus!" called a voice familiar, though wracked with age, from the top of the staircase. The old ventriloquist took the stairs carefully, silently, as the dogs turned and trotted off.

"Who the hell are you?" he said, sounding more curious than angry. He was tall with sloping shoulders not unlike those of his dogs. Strands of long white hair littered his head. Veins stood out in his arms and forehead. What looked like tentacles fanned down his muscular neck. Geist didn't recognize the ventriloquist's face at all; the only familiar characteristic, save the commanding voice, was his imposing height.

"I am just a fan, I'm afraid," Geist said. "I saw your act when I was just a boy, and I have to say, it stuck with me. I can't shake it."

The old man's expression softened. "That was a long time ago," he muttered. For a moment, his eyes unfocused. Geist feared the man might collapse to the ground. Then he blinked and looked at Geist warmly. "Come in," he said. "Come in. Let me make you some tea. Toast? Would you like toast?"

"Tea would be grand," Geist said.

They sat in easy chairs in McCutcheon's book-lined study. The old ventriloquist had a fire going, and the snaps and cracks and the heat made Geist pleasantly sleepy, despite the anxious anticipation of seeing that goddamned dummy again . . . if McCutcheon still had the thing. McCutcheon stirred his tea with a long pinky finger. "Don't get old," he said. "I've lived far longer than I planned. It hurts to move. To get up from a chair. To drop something and be unable to bend to pick it up is a special variety of torture. It hurts to remember those things irretrievable. And it hurts to forget them. My brain is atrophying."

Geist nodded absently, holding his teacup under his chin.

McCutcheon sighed. "You didn't come here to listen to the depressive rambling of an old man," McCutcheon said. "You've come here for something specific. I'll bet I know what it is."

Geist leaned forward and said, "Tell me, sir . . . do you still have Mr. Alberich Bugbear?"

"I do," McCutcheon said. "Or rather, he still has me. For now."

"May I see him?"

McCutcheon pushed himself up from his chair, groaning. He exited the room with an exaggerated slowness, as though silently chastising Geist for making him get up. Geist's heart beat wildly in his chest. His stomach felt hollow. Moments passed. The two Dobermans trotted into the room and took their places on either side of the old man's chair. A black cat followed them and leapt onto the arm, and then the back, of the chair. It tucked its tail and paws under itself and stared at Geist with secretive green eyes. The stage was set.

The dummy walked in alone.

Geist had anticipated fear, but he was not prepared for this. His breath hitched. His heart stuttered and raced. A rasping squeal sounded down in his throat. He stood on trembling legs, heat spreading through his head, and backed away around the chair, putting it between him and the dummy. The dogs and cat regarded the dummy with equanimity. The dummy's eyebrows waggled. Its wooden hands clenched and unclenched. It panted, a little wooden tongue jutting and retreating, jutting and retreating. It went into a crouch, about to leap—Geist shrieked—and it collapsed to the floor. McCutcheon appeared in the doorway, his hands raised at neck-level. He lifted them, waggling his fingers, and the dummy stood again. It turned and crawled up the ventriloquist's front like a kitten and then turned and sat in his now folded arms, its legs dangling. Its face settled.

McCutcheon chuckled at Geist's shocked, fearful expression. "You live with someone long enough . . ." he said, sitting back in his chair, the dummy lolling as though it had never moved of its own accord. "You can see I've mastered my craft. I had him moving independently a long time ago. But I couldn't do it on stage. I'd have been dragged out into the streets and set on fire. I still would. In time, this sort of thing will be accepted as some kind of mechanical trickery. But not yet."

A look of fear sailed like a cloud across his face. "I can't always control him," the old ventriloquist said.

"I once moved a teacup a half inch," Geist said. His heartbeat was settling down, but he was afraid to let his eyes wander from the supine dummy. "I vomited and then fell into three straight days of dreamless sleep."

The ventriloquist shrugged. "Different constitutions," he said. "Different levels."

Geist thought. He *needed* to study this dummy. He needed to take it apart and examine it. Fighting every instinct, every urge to flee, he said, "Let me take him off your hands."

McCutcheon cocked and eyebrow and cracked his knuckles. "So now we've come to the reason for your visit. You're not a fan at all, are you? You want to perform with him. You think you'll make money, my son? What did I just tell you? They'll crucify you."

"I'm no performer," Geist said. "I want to study him . . . and then destroy him. Or . . . cage him. Whatever I want to do with him, I need him out of my nightmares. It's immaterial to you. Name your price, sir, and I will be on my way."

The dummy's head rose. It stared at Geist. The old man's eyes came alive. They slid over to regard the dummy and back to Geist. There was pleading in them. The dummy's eyes shot over—Geist could hear wood sliding against wood, and the impact when they hit the wall of the eye—and shot hellfire at McCutcheon. *Keep quiet,* those wooden eyes seemed to say.

The dummy put its hand on McCutcheon's groin and squeezed. "He's a real cut-up," McCutcheon said in a choked voice as he pried the small fingers apart and shoved the hand away. Geist summoned all his courage and stood. He strode over and grabbed the dummy by the back of the neck and pried it from McCutcheon's lap. He backed up and held the dummy as far away from his body as he could. Its arms swung, and its legs kicked. "Do you have glue?" Geist asked.

"Glue?"

"Any adhesive will do."

McCutcheon rose, again groaning. He lurched from the room. A low, angry growl emanated from somewhere inside the dummy. A wordless voice sounded in Geist's head, and pain throbbed in his temples and under his tongue. "Hurry!" he shouted.

Time stretched. Finally, McCutcheon came back in with a small bottle with a stopper. Geist squeezed out a drop onto his index finger and touched it to the dummy's forehead. "Surcease," he said. "Surcease and settle." He then recited the relevant passage from the *Libellus Vox Larvae.*

As he spoke, the dummy trembled. The pictures rattled on their hooks. Somewhere in the house, glass shattered. The dummy's eyes rolled up to the whites. The hissing fire faded from orange to white and shot furious sparks against the screen. The tin ceiling peeled at the corners. Strange, distorted human and wooden faces appeared in the middle of the room, undulating like bedsheets in a wild wind, baring yellow teeth, growing larger, overlapping, folding like origami and unfolding, crude and grotesque, eyeballs staring from nostrils, whiskers growing on oversized eyeballs, a profusion of tongues and their roots, fat ears chewing and slurping and nursing on stringy chins.

The whites of McCutcheon's eyes went red. His mouth trembled, and a high-pitched voice spoke. *I'm just playing. Let me play. Goddammit, man, I'm an* artist. *Let me make my art. Let me work my animal dummy. He's so much fun, especially now that death looms nearer. So malleable. I've shown him such sights, and he refuses to go mad.*

Geist twisted his fingers into impossible shapes and flung them apart. A torrent of syllables tumbled from his mouth, and dummy and ventriloquist collapsed as one. From both of their mouths, something oily and purple oozed.

A darkness, an edge, a shadow.

Pain shot through his chest, sailed through his arms and legs to the tips of his fingers and toes. It circled his stomach and plunged into his groin where it stirred like a splintery wooden spoon on fire. All pain, a body painted inside and out with fire and stone. He fled into a swirling tunnel to unconsciousness. He and the ventriloquist and the dummy lay in a skewed triangle. For a time, the ticking clock was the only sound to be heard.

Geist blinked awake, logy and nauseated. A wavering snore emanated from the sleeping ventriloquist, or possibly from the dummy—that, he assumed, was what woke him. He clambered to his feet and looked down at the pair. They were still, head to head, real hair and false intermingling, forming an arrow that pointed to the stairs. Geist ascended slowly, trying to minimize creaking, anything that might cause his hosts to stir. Lining the wall were pictures of McCutcheon as a much younger man. In one, he stood proudly with his arm around the shoulders of a woman in a flowered dress with a calm and knowing gaze. In another, he sat hunched over an ancient, gleaming black typewriter, a teacup steaming in the foreground, making him appear to work in a magical mist. In a third, he sat on a stool with the dummy in his lap, him looking down paternally, the dummy looking back, a false innocence in its expression. In yet another, he held the dummy upside down by the legs, coins falling from its outturned pockets in a blurry rain of silver.

A pipe-scented dim hall lined with doors, one slightly ajar. Geist entered. A simple bed sagged, unmade. Beside it, a melted candle and a glass of water sat on a modest table. Across the room was the writing desk Geist recognized from the picture, strewn with documents, the black typewriter scratched and dented, its keys dusty, its numbers and letters all but worn away. Behind a trifold oriental screen, Geist found the closet door, and within a steamer trunk covered in faded labels. He opened its clasps to find musty clothing, small, as for a child. He pulled out enough to make room for the dummy.

He arrived downstairs to find McCutcheon gone, the dummy still supine. He folded it into the trunk, its shoes bookending its head, and he fled, leaving the front door hanging open.

Outside the train windows was fathomless blackness, as though the train was rumbling through some alternate universe bereft of stars, of light. The lamps of the interior of the train were no match for the darkness; all was a gray-tinged sepia, blurred black at the edges. The few other riders sat silent and still, and nary a cough nor a throat-clearing disturbed the tableau. Geist shifted uncomfortably in his seat, afraid to let the ruffling of his clothing insult the silence. In the seat beside him sat the case. Afraid of the dummy as he was, he felt oddly guilty letting it ride encased, smothered in clothing, surely the darkness there similar to that outside the train.

Slowly, quietly, he opened the case, fighting revulsion and lingering fear. The dummy stared at him from between its shoes. Geist unfolded the legs and pulled it from its malodorous confines. He moved the bag to the empty seat in front of him, then sat the dummy in the aisle seat next to him. He considered. He stood and moved the dummy to the window seat and turned its head to look out the window. *I am going mad,* he thought.

What time is it? Shouldn't I be home by now? Geist looked to the window. His reflection loomed over the dummy's. Still no light. The dummy shifted its eyes upward. Its reflection locked eyes with Geist's, and for just a moment, Geist saw himself through the dummy's eyes, his eyebrows a tangle, his face aghast, distorted with fear, and then he was looking at McCutcheon's face in the frame of a bathroom mirror, swathed in steam, staring angrily, vengefully, his mouth moving, though there was no sound, and then he was back on the train with the dummy staring at him in the reflection, its mouth open, its teeth glinting sharp and homicidal. He shrieked.

Footsteps sounded, someone running. The other passengers remained deathly quiet: this silence somehow different in a way Geist could not put a name to. He feared they were dead, that the dummy had somehow killed them when Geist was hallucinating. And now he would kill . . .

The attendant stood by his seat. "Sir," he said, "is something the matter?" He spoke at a moderate volume, but it sounded loud to Geist, like the booming voice of some ancient, offended god.

"Just night terrors," Geist replied. He hesitated. "Dark," he said. "Is it always so dark on this line?"

"This dark and darker," came the attendant's reply. "Why, sometimes it's so goddamned overwhelmingly dark that one wonders how one holds on to one's sanity. One wonders if *they* aren't coming to overrun us all with typhoons made up of whirring, interlocking blades surrounding acid-filled stomachs. Imagine it. The world a grand, ugly feast, man and beast and vegetation naught but a vast meal for creatures unfathomable, cruel and voracious and hungry with no hope of ever being sated." He grinned at Geist, a mad grin, his chin swaying low. His gums were black and blistered, his teeth—white as boiled eggs—visible almost to the root.

Geist stammered, and a bell rang somewhere in the back of the car. The attendant's eyes grew wide. "Mister Boyle desires his tea," he said, and he was gone.

"He seemed nice," the dummy muttered in McCutcheon's voice.

Am I dreaming? Geist thought. *I am not. But . . . I can control this.*

He pictured the dummy collapsing, and damned if it didn't happen. Its body went limp, slid down into the seat, twitched once, and was still. He pictured the attendant coming back, and sure enough, the man appeared. "You know," Geist said, "I think I should like some tea my own self. Nothing for my smallish companion. And also . . . an apology."

The attendant's face softened. "I'm frightfully sorry if I was out of line, sir," he said, wringing his hands, true contrition in his watering eyes. "The dark . . . it gets to me."

"It gets to all of us," Geist said.

The train pitched downward and picked up speed. The other passengers did not gasp, did not move, not that Geist could hear or detect. Outside the window, a red phosphorescence leaked into the black like blood into ink. Far off, the blackness separated itself into furrowed, wriggling forms, like maggots made from coal. Long fingers began to push themselves out, followed by distorted faces.

"*STOP THIS!*" bellowed Geist. The trajectory of the train evened out, went horizontal. Outside the window, all went a dusky blue. The lights of the city blinked and then shone strong. Buildings and roads swum into being, then rain, then people, moving through the drizzling rain, hunched under frowning black umbrellas.

The dummy lay in pieces on the carpet. A straight-lined wooden spine with brass levers. The head, face down. The back opened like double-doors, inside a tangle of coiled wires and pulleys. The arms and legs. The small hands and feet placed in a stained-glass ramekin like baby mice. Geist sat cross-legged in his wine-stained robe. "You're not frightening," he insisted, "and I'm not frightened."

The dummy's head shook with tremors. The levers on the spine flicked up and down. The hands and feet clenched and unclenched, clinking in the ramekin. Geist trembled. "You're not . . ." He rose and exited the room.

What to do? Do I burn it? What if it can regenerate? How much of McCutcheon is in there—if I destroy the dummy, will I destroy him as well?

An hour later, he re-entered the room, having meditated on the matter, having consulted with various oracles both human and otherwise. He took up the dummy's parts in a basin and brought them to the washroom. Its torso and clothing he cleansed with warm water and detergent; its plastic flesh he wiped down with a cloth damp with antiseptic cleansers. Then he reassembled the dummy until it was as close to new as could be managed without a professional restoration. He placed it on a chair in his study, arranging it just so. He would spend his days and his nights in its company. He would watch its face for movement, stare into its unseeing eyes as a contest. Maybe then the dreams would cease.

They did not.

But just as on the train, Geist could control them. He could send the dummy skyward until it was a small black star, blacker than the space into which it had been launched. He could will it into all-consuming flames. He could humiliate it, dropping its pants and revealing its featureless crotch.

After a time, he felt bad for the poor thing. After a time, he made his peace with it.

And then the nightmares did indeed cease.

Decades, centuries, aeons. An eternity of nihil. No one floats in nowhere. His awareness of his own nascent being blossoms slowly over decades. It reaches fruition at no-time, its non-hands passing through nothing. Days, weeks, years. Then a change. Something from nothing. Nature's scofflaw. A yellow blur in the blackness, undulating, blinking, fading, seething. The blink of life may as well never have happened. He is drowned in an inkwell of forgetting, the black murk of nonexistence. The fat man at the centermost round table hushes the ladies with a dark glance to his left and to his right. The whole restaurant goes mute as though we've put our hands over our ears. The man regards the cook. Watch his brow lower, his countenance darken, his fat, liver-spotted fists clench, his beard burgeon like a storm cloud. You see it in his eyes. I see it too. This will not come easily, he's thinking. There will be a struggle.

Yes, the old man is rising, leaping to the surface of his table, slicing through the greasy air with his cane, now throwing it into the air like a swordsman, catching it, pointing at this and that diner patron as though offering blessings. Now he's kicking the plates off the table. He certainly has *my* attention.

"Gentlemen," Walter said, "and ladies. And all in-between and on either side. I want to welcome you to the show you didn't know about, the resurrection, the dawn of a new Leeds, a demon's dream, a shared hallucination from which we shall never awake. Some of you will play a role. The others will provide an audience of witnesses. No one will be the same.

"You may call me Walter. With apologies to the restaurant staff, I will be taking over as host for the remainder of the evening."

Walter's women stand and throw their chairs to the floor. It's a needless gesture, sure, but it's theater. Presentation is always important. Sometimes presentation is everything. Now they're going around and pulling chairs from empty tables, transforming the dining room into a makeshift amphitheater with rows of chairs, fan-shaped and facing the table on which Walter Clough stands, arms crossed. At their direction, the wait staff, cowed and quiet, stacks the tables in front of the doors.

"Sir, why don't you stand up?"

Bill Valerio had returned from the bathroom, having puked out his last several meals and a quart or so of blood-threaded bile. A ghost of nausea remained, so he'd been sitting quietly, concentrating on getting past it, so much so that the commotion had gone on without his having paid any heed. Now hearing this loud voice cut across the diner, he looks to see the old, bearded man standing on his table. The man stares right at him . . . *through* him. Feeling like an idiot, he points at himself. "Me?"

"Well, who else?"

Bill extracts himself from the booth and stands.

"Ladies and gentlemen, I'd like to introduce Bill Valerio. Bill's had a bitch of a day, drifting on a dark river of nightmares, pursued like so much quarry . . . but he made it here in one piece. And I see he's brought a little friend. Bring him over, why don't you?"

Bill looks at the seat to his left. The dummy, still under his jacket, has stood somehow, though its legs have no discernible interior structure, just polyester stuffed with felt. Bill pulls the jacket away. The dummy's large blue eyes coldly survey the room. It parts its upsettingly sensual painted-pink lips, revealing a leering smile full of Chiclet teeth.

Bill leans, hoists the dummy up by its armpits, holding it as far away from his body as possible, and walks over to the old man's table. He hands the dummy up like an offering. Walter receives it with a wink, kisses it on the forehead, goes down to one knee, and rests the dummy gently, almost lovingly, onto the table, arranging its arms at its side and straightening its slack legs. Bill hastens back to his booth, relieved to be free of the thing. It had had a new, unexpected heft to it and had felt loathsome in his hands, like a damp bag full of vipers.

Jabin creeps from the kitchen and crouches on the mat behind the register, the chef's knife gripped tightly in his hand. He prays silently. From this vantage, he can see just the man's torso and head. Doubt assails him with the unexpected suddenness of a tap on the shoulder in an empty room. There will be no resurrection, *can* be no resurrection. It's impossible. That flesh could somehow be conjured up from trifles spread out on a diner table, never mind internal organs, a skeleton, a thinking brain—it is impossibility and insanity itself. It cannot happen.

Can it?

He will watch and wait and let the Lord guide his hand. Guide his blade. He looks at it, glinting in the fluorescent light. It isn't *the* knife, but it is *a* knife. It is sharp, can slice through flesh, hack into bone, defying resistance. In the absurd event that he'll have to wield it, it will do what it was meant to do. That settled, he kneels and waits.

"Ma'am?" Walter calls.

Jeannine looks up from her plate. Her lips are sticky with barbecue sauce. Stains smear her blouse. The bearded man on the table wants her for something, and all she wants to do is shrink back into her seat and just . . . fall away. She misses Missy and Miles, misses Frank, misses the dog. All she wants is to take to her bed. Failing that, she wants to disappear, be done with it, done with everything, the whole mess.

The thought occurs to her that she's lost her mind. She conjures up this scenario almost too easily. It is simple and plausible and comforting. She hadn't gotten lost in the woods, hadn't seen that horrid thing in the clearing nor met up with some evil couple with a . . . *fluctuating* pregnancy—rather, she'd lost her darn marbles. Missy and Miles had returned to find her unconscious in the leaf-domed grotto where she'd gone to relieve herself. They'd called 911, had her airlifted to a hospital room in Cooley Dickinson. She is there, really, not here. She's reclined on a bed in the ICU in a coma with a tube in her mouth and an IV in her arm, surrounded by machines. She thinks that if she listens hard, beyond this hideous hallucinated nightmare, she'll hear them calling to her, saying, *Mom, wake up. Come back to us. We love you.*

"Ma'am, won't you come over here for just a moment?"

Her reverie broken, Jeannine exits the booth with exaggerated difficulty, sighing and groaning, splaying her fingers on the tabletop. Finally up, she raises her hands in the air, palms up.

"What?" she snaps.

"Bring your bag, please."

She moans theatrically, snatches the duffel from the booth, and hauls it over to the table. Walter grabs it roughly from her hands, pulling out the thermos and spice jars. He regards them, pleased, and puts them aside for the moment. He starts pulling other things out, throwing them at her. A tube of antacid tablets flies over her left shoulder. A hairbrush caroms off the side of her head, trailed by wadded up tissues and loose change. "Back to your booth, you cranky old broad," he says as Jeannine cries out.

"Now you," he says, pointing at the businessman.

At some point while he'd been pouring tepid coffee through a gooey red gauntlet of half-chewed cherry pie, Dave Strell lost his ever-loving mind. It snapped like the stem of a dry, dead leaf. He was now decidedly a few sandwiches, a pitcher of lemonade, a basket, a blanket, and a grassy hillock short of a picnic.

He grins a cherry-filling grin when the white-bearded man hops up on the diner table and begins to work the crowd. Strell claps his hands brainlessly, connecting most of the time, and then jams his pinky fingers into the sides of his mouth, producing just a whispering hiss instead of the shrill whistle he'd been going for. An acidic mélange of his meal bubbles up in his throat and dribbles down his chin. "Whooooooo," he rasps.

When a short time later Walter sends the old woman away, hurling junk from her bag at her hunched, retreating form, Dave feels some atavistic need to defend her or avenge her or at least *say something*. When Walter calls to him like an airport worker hailing someone over a loudspeaker—"*STRELL . . . MISTER DAVID STRELL*"—he just stares until finally a long-legged blonde strides over and hauls him up by his collar. She raises one eyebrow and jams her hand into Dave's front pants pocket. He gasps. When she pulls her hand back out, he sighs. She opens her fist to reveal the rings she'd retrieved and goes back to the table. Dave watches her go. His mouth is very dry. He tries to moisten it with his tongue to no avail. He dribbles and gibbers and paws at himself. His bowels and bladder empty themselves into his Dockers.

Walter touches his index finger to the dummy's bottom lip and lowers its jaw. He rubs the spices onto its wooden tongue and lips, pushing them down its throat and swirling his fingertips around its cheeks. Carla separates and splays the fingers of its hands, and Leeza slides the rings onto the plastic fingers.

Carla then pulls from her bag a large, ancient book. It looks out of place in the diner, and rightfully so; its proper home is the third shelf down on the left-most set of shelves in the rare books room of the Leeds Public Library, a spot from which it was, as the note in a slip of paper in its hinge indicates in unequivocal ALL CAPS, never to be removed under penalty of immediate termination and aggressive legal action. She opens it to the middle pages and recites a passage in a bygone tongue.

Leeza stands next to her and begins to speak as well, their voices overlapping here, meshing there, until they speak in one voice. Walter joins in, his voice the clear and unalloyed baritone of a much younger man. The triad of voices, declaiming like a song sung in rounds, forms a new language, or a very old one. The lights in the diner go red, and the sprinklers twitch to life and spray brackish pink water down on the ceremony and on the diners. Walter raises his arms. His hands sprout more fingers; they burst from his palm, from his wrist and forearm, from the back of his hand, from between the other fingers. They move in complex patterns like storm-lashed, denuded trees. His many nails extend into claws.

"The dummy!" shouts Bill Valerio, and the assembled throng, who had been staring unblinking at the trio, gasp as one. The surface of the dummy's tuxedo-clad body bubbles like water on the boil, the body elongating as though being pulled taut on a rack. Cracks appear in its veneered head to reveal wet pinkish flesh shot through with blue veins. Chips of its furrowed hair and veneered skin crumble like chalk and spill to the tabletop. The rings on its fingers shed their decades of dirt and grime; brown clouds rise from their surfaces and dissipate in the whirling ceiling fans. The rings gleam and glow in a spectral miasma.

As the trio continues its wicked rhapsodic chant, the dummy sits bolt upright.

It is now taller, more filled-in. Its face ripples wildly. Lines form and widen into furrows. The dummy hisses, louder and louder, building, and finally both eyes pop out like bullets. One of them shoots through the front window.

Upon impact, a hot wind howls through the Look Diner like the depressurized interior of an airplane, sending napkins and menus and food whipping around the room like frenzied ghosts. Simultaneously, the other eye shoots straight through Bill Valerio's forehead, leaving a half-dollar-sized hole above his left brow. The glass eye bounces wildly around the interior of Bill's skull until it breaks into curved shards that puree his brain. The contents of his skull pour like over-watered oatmeal from his nostrils and mouth, followed by torrents of blood. The front of his skull collapses inward, his face folding into itself like a deflating balloon, and he slides under the table dead.

Jabin watches the proceedings in horror, frozen in place. The women guarding the table are as watchful and wary as ivory-fanged hounds guarding a beloved master. He needs their attention diverted before he makes his move—but now *he's* the one distracted, shocked as the dummy pries swatches of wood from its face, as its clothes stretch out and its shoes split open, as liquid white, blue, and black pool in its newly vacant sockets, forming human eyes. The witches are now bellowing so that the words of their spell can be heard over the howling wind by whatever hideous demons they're calling. Leeza unfolds a blue robe and drapes it over the dummy as it quickly outgrows its miniature outfit.

Something pops and clatters in the kitchen behind Jabin, and he whips around to see the pans on the burners grow blossoms of flame. They reach like orange fingers to touch the ceiling. When he turns back around, a blue-robed man with bright-red skin stands where the dummy had been, arms outstretched, rings glinting on his fingers. Geist. The women fall to their knees before him, their hands up in worship, their eyes squeezed shut. It has to be now before this goes any further. Through the cacophony, Jabin approaches, gripping the knife, white-knuckled. With his left hand, he grabs a fluttering napkin from midair, dunks it in a glass of water on a table, and holds it over his mouth and nose.

Dave Strell sees a wiry man in dog's tooth chef pants and a black T-shirt, striding purposefully from the kitchen, black smoke billowing behind him, a large knife in his fist, a napkin over his face. The need to intervene again floods his addled brain. Here is his chance—no one else has seen the man. "*Knife!*" he yells as he grabs the cherry-pie-stained fork and charges at Jabin.

The man who Walter had called *Something* Strell came as if from nowhere, holding a fork out before him, angling toward Jabin, moving quickly, trying to block Jabin's access to the table where the triumvirate of witches stares rapturously at their newly resurrected master. As Jabin picks up his pace, a little too late, the women's eyes leap open, their heads swivel to size up the threat. Strell intercepts Jabin just before the table, holding the fork straight out in front of him, staring with a strange look in his eyes, a mix of triumph, righteous outrage, and confusion.

Strell jabs ineffectually at the hollow of Jabin's throat. Jabin grabs his wrist and twists until a dull snap sounds. He hurls Strell to the ground and holds him there with his heel on Strell's temple. The ladies leap at Jabin. He struggles forward, punching and kicking, feeling their teeth in his neck and their nails tearing at the tender flesh of his stomach, as Strell crawls away on his belly like a great pale reptile in khakis, holding his wounded hand up over his head. Jabin frees himself from the women's clutches and thrusts the knife straight into Geist's throat. The blade curls like cardboard. It doesn't so much as make a mark. Carla grabs the knife by its blade and throws it blindly. It shoots into the back of Dave Strell's neck, stilling him forever.

Carla kicks at Jabin's calves until he loses his footing and falls to the floor, and the two ladies set upon him. Carla digs a long press-on fingernail into his eye socket as Leeza chews hard into his armpit. He screams for his God, and from the periphery of his vision swim translucent angels, looking for all the world like the Sea-Monkeys on the package he'd had as a child—round bellies, angular cheeks, stalks atop their heads, expressions of bemusement on their faces. Fluttering slowly, dreamlike despite the howling winds, they look benevolent—glinting, shimmering harbingers of goodness.

He struggles to rise, pushing up on his elbows. Through the angelic cellophane bodies, his eyes catch sight of a pair of men sitting at the corner table: one of them nondescript, a cipher in dark glasses with a wooden white cane in his fist, the other a skeletal man in a loose-fitting shirt with a tangle of gray-brown hair clinging to his dome-like skull, his eyes rolling loose in his sockets, held in by a pinkish miasma of gelatin. The cadaverous man makes eye contact with Jabin and holds aloft the darkly enchanted knife that Jabin had lost. Jabin's eyes widen.

Such chaos, isn't it. I always like a show with my dinner. Helps with digestion. And this is quite the rave-up. I appreciate that you've joined me. I brought something with me. A surprise. Right here in this box. It's the knife. *The* knife. And you've been wondering exactly who I am, I'm sure. They call me Mister White Noise. I'm the chaos in the magic, the white leech in the bathtub basin, the deus in the machina, and I hate an unfair fight.

The skeletal man speaks briefly to his companion, stands, grasps the edge of the table with one withered hand for balance, and throws the knife to Jabin. End over end it spins, drawing a black-and-silver roulette wheel as it arcs across the restaurant, missing one of the ceiling fans by a fraction of a millimeter. Jabin sees it in slow motion, *everything* in slow motion, the flying knife, the ceiling fans, the whirling napkins, the fleeing waitresses, all moving at a stunted, jerky crawl, and he struggles to his feet and holds his hand up as far as it could go, stretching his arm until his muscles burn, even as the godless harridans clutching at him dig their brown teeth into his armpit and side, tearing open the tender skin, chewing wildly at muscle and fat. He catches the knife in his fist, angles the blade downward, and lets it drop. It sinks into the crown of the blonde's head like a diver into water. As Leeza crumples to the ground, Carla puts a foot on her shoulder and wrenches the knife from her head. Jabin and Carla scramble to their feet. She stands, legs apart, thrusting the knife as Jabin weaves and feints. They circle one another warily, stepping over Leeza's prone body. Carla's jaw drops, and her eyes widen as the knife's haft begins to glow red. She tosses it from hand to hand and then lets it go. Jabin grabs the haft as it falls. Blisters bubble and steam on Carla's palm.

Something is wrong with our resurrected occultist, isn't it? He's swaying slightly, watching the action in a daze. It's not just that he's newly back from nowhere. Something irrevocable has occurred in him. Something is wrong with his eyes, something strange in how his hands move over the surface of his head as though he's trying to find the worms within, using just the tips of his fingers. He tries to wet his lips, but his tongue is a dry, bristly thing, white as though with frost or fungus. His breathing is labored, his stance troubling. There's violence in it, and irrationality. A fog of wrongness, a miasma of unreality surrounds him. A violation of nature as profound as has ever been. The repercussions are unthinkable.

Never mind what phantasms the dead may dream—what of the dreams of the undead, dreams that can reshape reality, dreams of a resurrected monster of a man gone mad from a tour at the cups of eternity's black spiral?

"This is against God," Shantaya says. She and Marci stand surrounded by sheet-pan racks, like giants in a city center. Marci pulls a cast-iron skillet from a hook. She looks at it and up at Shantaya's face, wan and covered in sweat. "How good is *your* throwing arm?" she says.

"How good is your throwing arm?"

"It's been three weeks since my wrist arthroscopy. And one of us is in a softball team . . . and it's not me."

"Shit." Shantaya snatches up the skillet. "Who do I throw it at, the fat guy or the puppet guy in the robe?"

"I'm going to take a wild guess and say that, if you take out the fat guy, whatever's happening with the puppet will stop." She grins helplessly. "If you told me this morning that I'd be saying that sentence tonight . . ."

She walks toward the dining room. No one is looking in her direction. When she reaches the threshold, she raises the skillet over her head and considers . . . she trusts her ability to throw underhand just a little bit more. She swings the skillet by her side in increasing arcs, letting momentum build, and lets it fly.

Jeannine looks down at the dead man with the knife in his neck, leaking blood onto the scattered change and crumpled napkins and tissues. She slides from the booth and kneels quietly at the man's side. Trying not to whimper, she places one hand on the back of the man's head—it's startlingly cold—and with the other she slides out the chef's knife. With some difficulty, she stands and creeps toward where the white-haired cook and the brunette stripper tussle over the glowing knife. She lets loose a wavering cry and stabs the hollow between the woman's shoulder blades.

She's wide of the mark; the knife penetrates the skin at the woman's left shoulder and hits bone. The woman screams and elbows blindly behind her, catching Jeannine in the jaw. Jeanine stumbles backward, wailing, and freezes—something is sailing through the air at her. She can't make sense of the thing. Fleetingly, she sees it as a great black owl with shining talons, cruel eyes, and a pointed black beak. Then it fills her vision, an expanding inkblot. It crashes into her nose and mouth, sending teeth scattering, caving her face in horizontally. She gulps in vain for air, staring up at the fading ceiling light, her hands clawing at nothing. Blurred heads crane over her. "Missy?" she says. "Miles?" Then Frank is floating above her—her Frank, looking just as he did as a young man, broad-chested, hair in a crew cut. But something is wrong with his face. His tongue lolls, and his teeth are long and pointed. His eyeballs are polished black marbles. His body splits wide open, his rib cage expanding, his torn-up sides becoming wings, his legs and arms shrinking, blackening, his nails pinching inward, becoming claws. He screeches like some great prehistoric bird and flies up into the gulfs of blackness above. She reaches for him and realizes that, as he rises, she's falling, falling fast. The light shrinks to a pinprick in a coal-black eternity and blinks out forever.

Walter Clough watches the heavy, cast-iron pan pass by his face and take out the old lady. He gasps and then applauds vigorously, his face reddening, as the two waitresses who'd thrown the thing flee shrieking back from whence they'd come. He jumps down from the table, pain shooting up his calves and exploding in his knees. He falls heavily into his chair. His limbs feel weighted down, his skin hot and damp. He holds up his fingers. They are unrecognizable as his own. Swollen and pink.

Before him, Geist is unfolding, unfurling, becoming real again. Leeza—poor Leeza—is down, but Carla has the chef well in hand. She's a beast, a fighter, a monster. Walter knows that now he must take a back seat to the proceedings. His voice had been essential for the spell to work, but now, that done, his role is necessarily diminished. He longs simultaneously to sit quietly with Geist at a restaurant table somewhere and resume their relationship and also to fall into a deep, dark sleep in the cool shadows of his chamber. Neither can happen yet. Once Geist is whole again, Walter is to spirit him, along with the women, away to Anne Gare's basement. He and Anne have set everything up nicely for his recovery. Once Geist is there and comfortable, Walter can finally return to his home atop Round Hill Road and collapse into his bed.

Nothing. Then something. Hazy light, blurred figures and muted colors moving in all directions. A triad of voices, distant and muted. He feels coldness in the shape of a body, a hard surface pressing on his back and buttocks and calves. His brain sends signals outward, and he feels his own arms move. Something stings where his eyes should be, and he finds them with his fingers and wipes away something viscous and oily. He opens them now. All is still a blur. He digs the gunk out from under his nose, and aromas work their way in—burnt bacon, toast, roasted beef, coffee, and singed hair. He wipes at his ears, and the sounds of a struggle work their way in, voices familiar and unfamiliar, grunts and cries, a whipping wind carrying some sounds away and bringing others tantalizingly close.

"Mother? Father?" He half expects to open his eyes to find that old familiar kitchen, steam rising from the stovetop, his mother smiling her brilliant smile, his father's hand landing on the back of his neck and giving his hair a rough, loving tousling. Then the one-two punch of that long-ago loss slams into him yet again, followed by a juggernaut of memories, the darkness and light of his nights and days flashing at him like a strobe light. Priests weeping and begging, shadows in the woods, cadavers in colonial clothing filling a lamp-lit city road, the green glow of a radio dial, great holes in the earth, and a globular sun mutating over a scorched, savage land. Darkness and the things writhing there. Living strings

of abomination shoot through his brain and squeeze into knots. He laughs and weeps and gibbers.

He climbs to his feet and jumps from the table to the carpeted floor where a wiry man in chef's clothing awaits, wielding a glowing knife.

As Carla reaches back to assess the damage to her shoulder, Jabin drops himself to the ground, one leg on either side of Carla's feet. He scissors his legs at her ankles and her balance goes. Her back hits the floor, and then her head, a loud percussion you can feel in your feet. She's still conscious but dazed and in throbbing pain. Walter cries out and jumps from his chair and is almost overtaken by a wave of dizziness and nausea. He can't let the cook get to Geist. He advances, and the world wavers and goes gray. The cook lunges at him.

The world blinks black for a fraction of a millisecond.

And Walter is sitting on the floor, his legs splayed out before him. He doesn't know how he got there. A great wind still blows through the restaurant, but everyone is in a frozen tableau. Napkins hang in the air like shards of exploded ghosts. Geist is a robed statue. The other diners are standing, their mouths an array of black circles like bubbles of ink. Some blurred thing looms in his lower periphery. He looks down. A piece of wood is growing from his beard. He tugs at it, but it's stuck. Dull pain spreads through his throat and billows in his chest. He tries again. His beard goes bright red and spits sodden streamers of red onto his legs, onto the floor. A tingle goes through his body, and he has a notion so very curious . . . he feels as though he's coated in sand. His eyes widen, and for just a flash, he looks like that awestruck little boy, seated in wide-eyed wonder across from Geist for the first time at a post-christening ceremony. His crown and forehead crumple and turn to white-beige powder. It spills down over his eyes, into his red beard, lands like an avalanche on the great round hill of his gut. Then red powder pours like sindoor from his open mouth as his insides dry and crumple. His skeleton breaks apart, and he collapses to the carpet. Jabin kneels and touches the powder to his finger, raises that finger to his tongue and tastes it. The taste is familiar.

"*Body of Christ?*" Geist says. Jabin looks up at that white face so recently just dust, reborn into the world.

"Abrecan Geist," Jabin says.

"Is that me?" Geist says. "Or am I . . . Andrew?" He is addlepated and adrift but coiled like a viper, trembling with stored energy. Bits of chipped wood adorn his plastered-down hair, and sawdust gilds the shoulders of his robe. "I'm me," he says, sounding unsure. "But who are you?"

"I'm here in the service of God," Jabin says. "To send you back to hell."

A light comes on somewhere behind Geist's eyes. He scoffs. "Dial it down a notch, son. There is no such place. One of the more absurd and unimaginative manifestations of Christian guilt." He wipes his thumb down the corners of his mouth. "I was nowhere. Nowhere at all."

"You were . . . in hell's anteroom." Doubt clouds Jabin's face. The glow in his knife fades to a dim nimbus of yellow.

Geist points at it, grinning. "You got sold a bill of goods," he says. "That knife is no more magical than a Wüsthof cheese knife. Please tell me it runs on belief. Because yours is weak. Come on, bargain-counter holy man. Thrift store saint. Your God is dead or fled. It's just me and you now. A devil and a man. No God to intervene on your behalf. You've wasted your life."

Geist tilts his head. "Tell me. Why didn't you become a priest? Unworthy of the collar? What are you hiding behind that frowning face? Common lust? Rage? The instinct to murder? Or is it something darker? Something forbidden? Ah, that's it. I can see it in your expression." His face warps into a cruel parody of sympathy. "The girl on the floor, there, the one poor Walter brought, the blonde with blood pooling under her body. That's the way you like them, no? Half-dressed and unresponsive? A little time for acrobatic fun before the rigor mortis kicks in? Do you like them best when they can't talk back?

"Let it out. It's just me and you.

"You pervert."

Jabin plants the knife in the center of Geist's chest. Geist's eyes widen. He falls to his knees. He gurgles and sputters. His eyes close, and his torso sways. Jabin blinks.

And Geist begins to snore softly.

He isn't dying . . . but falling asleep.

Geist raises a serene face skyward. With a wet slurp, the knife sinks a little further. Another slurp and it's pulled in, gone, leaving a bright red gash. Geist gurgles like a newborn. His chest and neck heave. Then the tip of the blade peeks from Geist's grimacing mouth, pointing at the ceiling. The wound on his chest closes, fades red to pink, pink to white. The knife blade swells. Wet black feathers pour from its surface as its tip becomes a yellow beak. It struggles from Geist's throat, twisting its body until it is free. On shaking, twig-like legs, it takes a few uneasy steps across the bridge of Geist's nose and onto his forehead. It shakes its body, and feathers fly, get caught in the wind, fill the air. Yellow stripes appear on the crow, and it fattens further. Its body convulses and constricts just below its neck and just above its legs. A black, barbed stinger grows out from its tail. Then more legs pop out like black worms being birthed. Its eyes bulge and blacken like the bellies of tumors. Its wings are now translucent, fluttering madly as it flies up to the ceiling.

The assembled diners, in a thrall-borne imitation of Geist, raise their faces to the ceiling in unison. Their lips loosen and flatten and separate and expand, covering their faces like wet petals. Their tongues slither up from their mouths like snakes. Their bodies wither to stalks. Thorns burst from their dwindling limbs. The great bee-crow sails down and flits from human flower to human flower, slurping greedily from mouth after mouth. Green grass sprouts from the carpet below as the human flowers sway.

Jabin crouches and leaps, climbs the resurrected madman like a tree.

Geist staggers back as Jabin's hands encircle his throat. His eyes become candy-colored lollipops, spinning wildly in their sockets. Red glitter explodes like fireworks from his ears and mouth. He puts his fists to his sides and roars. Knife blades pop from his body like the quills of a porcupine, from his arms, his legs, his chest and back. Jabin's eyes go wide as countless blades perforate his body, lancing through muscle and organ and bone. The two are, for a moment, frozen in a bloody embrace. Then Geist leans forward and lets the cook slide to the floor. He kneels at the bleeding man's side. "I'm going to dream you into an eternity of blackness," he says. "And you'll be conscious. Call it God's love."

Jabin, laying on his back, looks to the table from where the skeletal man with gelatin eyes had thrown him the knife, but the table is empty, cleared and clean. *Dead or fled.* He tilts back his head and looks at Geist. The great bee-crow has returned to its creator. From its distended belly, tubular teats sway. Geist gathers them with fat hands, crowds them into his mouth, and slurps at them like a calf, his tongue swirling, his throat pulsing.

Geist's voice caroms around Jabin's head. *This is death. This is eternity. The life of the planet is a millionth of a blink. Millions and billions of years. Maybe you can find your God in there. What would he look like, do you think? Some creature from a thousand fathoms deep is my guess. Translucent skin, grotesque eyes on gelatinous stalks. Many-jointed, barbed arms. Serrated pincers and long, tusk-like teeth that curve over a misshapen, lumpy head. Though the darkness hides me. Tentacles and tendrils with glowing bulbs at their tips. God of power and might, piercing souls in the watery heavens, heaven and earth are full of your glory, and burying them in the dirt at the bottom of the word, clouds of...*

And the voice fades, and everything fades and is replaced by nothing. Jabin sees it, hears it, feels it all, an eternity of space and of time, one eternity atop the other, a funhouse mirror facing a funhouse mirror, forever and ever, amen.

The Lincoln Town Car sails up North King Street, on one side the state forest looming, on the other closed businesses squat in empty parking lots bathed in pools of LED light. Geist groans in the reclined passenger seat. Carla looks over at him with concern, his creased face blue from the dashboard lights, and then back at the road. He snorts, sighs, and rolls over onto his side. Then he snores softly, a cat-like purr, contented.

We are now in a ceiling-less corridor of dim-lit residences and farmland, the forest rising on either side and closing in behind us like ash-blackened double doors. Slimy things move among the trees, snaking under the roots and around the trunks and through the branches. The shadows on the moon shift, and it deflates and goes a curdled, pale brown. The stars begin to blink rapidly as though air-starved, and they shoot shimmering webs each to each, dividing the darkness into a million strangely shaped shards.

The white lines leap from the pavement and swim like mad wraiths around the car. They knock on the windows until the glass cracks and sprouts spiderweb fissures.

And the wheels adhere to the dermis of the road and peel it up, flinging it away in great, thin shreds and tendrils, revealing necrotized flesh, purple-ringed black bloody caverns, red gelatinous gore upon which great yellow grubs feast in countless numbers. O the nauseous noises of their chewing! O their insatiable hunger! Each one a god! Each one a paean to unthinkable beauty! Pungent, mephitic gases bubble up through yellow, boiling fat. Fissures widen, revealing seething, reeking decay. Rot holds sway. The road and the chewed-up world fall away. The car doors open, rise, become great wings. It flies up into skies teeming with long-fanged, finned tumors with horror show eyes, worms the length of a thousand stacked skyscrapers, clusters of green-glowing spores, tangles of muck-sotted hair in flocks, cadavers doing the breaststroke, capes of flayed flesh floating behind them.

It's late, so late. Almost three, hours from dusk and hours till dawn. A police car with LEEDS and TO SECURE AND TO AID emblazoned on the side turns from Main onto Maple. A stained Styrofoam Dunkin' cup sits, lid off, in the cup holder, about an inch of cooling coffee remaining. The laptop on the dash plays eighties rock hits. The car smells of vanilla and perspiration.

Officer Terrence Chenette is at the wheel: four years a beat cop now, too young to truly know the horrors of having lived through the eighties, barely able to grow a respectable mustache. He calls himself a night owl. Jokes that he can't sleep when there's injustice in the world. Truth is, he just can't sleep, injustice notwithstanding. Hasn't gotten more than an hour at a time in weeks. And for the past few weeks, those hours have been so stuffed full of strange and disquieting dreams that he might as well have been awake. His body aches from what it endures in his dreams.

In one recurrent nightmare, he's running on a white hamster wheel suspended in the still air of a blue-lit cavern. Craggy walls sit still and silent in the blurred distance, up and down as far as the eye can see. A black wheel, also spinning, approaches him. Someone's running on that wheel, someone with many arms that wriggle and writhe. It's too dark to make out the features. The black wheel accelerates. When the two wheels clash, white hot sparks erupt. He tumbles through the bent spokes and into those terrible, curling arms. In another, he rises from the toilet, looks back to see that it's full of eggs. Things are hatching from them. The cracks in the eggs never open wide enough for him to see what's emerging.

Not long left on his shift now, so he stops thinking about his dreams, lets himself instead picture Sarah: sprawled in the sheets of their bed, red hair tied up in an unruly bun, face creased with worry. The lot of a cop's wife, even though he's never had to draw his service revolver, never had even so much as a foot chase. The closest he's come to death was in a squalid apartment a few miles out of the city center, administering naloxone to a dreadlocked white boy in the throes of overdose. A deep scratch on his arm from the kid's filthy fingernail, the kid's saliva slathered on the wound. An AIDS test, sweating it out for a couple of extremely long weeks. Negative. Phew. Life in the small city goes on. Frivolous 911 calls about voices on the radio or winged old men in the treetops. The occasional beer-fueled domestic dust-up. Missing kids, mostly from well-to-do families, probably runaways. Taking in some lunatic shouting at the traffic about doom and devilry and dark times coming down.

But yes, let that all fall away and consider Sarah. Respite and rest and comfort. Soon he'll be sliding into those sheets, smelling her hair and her exhaustion. He picks up the cup, sips, grimaces. The sky is a strange purple, he notices, with tinges of crimson and yellow. He rolls down the side window and looks up. Something's moving above the clouds, zigzagging and gathering in their masses. Hard to tell exactly what.

He glances at the city block to his right, and the bookstore's all lit up as though it's the middle of the day. People move among the shelves, shadows spilling onto the walk. Some kind of party maybe. This late though? The word *homecoming* flashes in his brain.

Something hits his windshield with a splat. Strange, clear gelatin shot through with green veins. Something else, something heavy, crashes down on the roof of his cruiser. He hears the light bar shatter. The ceiling crumples in. He pulls over and gets out of the car. He can't make any sense of what's sprawled across the roof, blocky and many-limbed. Like a mix of crab and fern and bear and human and . . . armoire? The sky creaks like an old house, and the light changes, goes purplish. Chenette looks up at the bulging, cracking sky. The clouds have folded over, revealing a sky full of hamster wheels and strange winged things and a deep and endless well full of that which should not be. He sees a grotesque cluster of eggshells, cracking wide open, releasing what he had not yet been shown in his dreams, and his mouth opens wide and wider. You'd never know a mouth could open so wide. Officer Terrence Chenette eats the newly waking world of nightmares and is eaten.

§

Matthew M. Bartlett was born in 1970 in New England, where Halloween casts a darkly luminous shadow that outstretches its season. His 2014 out-of-nowhere self-published debut, *Gateways to Abomination*, launched a writing career that includes mosaic novels, short story collections, spoken-word records, and stories published in a variety of anthologies and journals, including *Forbidden Futures*, *Vastarien*, *Year's Best Weird Fiction Vol. 3*, *Cosmic Horror Monthly*, and others. In late 2020, in the heat of the New Pestilence, with vaccines just a glow on the horizon, he joined the Great Resignation, immediately launching his current ongoing project, now in its third year: a subscription service for monthly illustrated chapbooks, entitled the *WXXT Program Guide*. He writes and sells books and booze at various outlets in Western Massachusetts. He lives in Easthampton with his wife Katie Saulnier (whose art graces the cover of *Gateways to Abomination*) and their cats Peachpie and Larry.

BROKEN EYE BOOKS

Sign up for our newsletter at
www.brokeneyebooks.com

Welcome to Broken Eye Books! Our goal is to bring you the weird and funky that you just can't get anywhere else. We want to create books that blend genres and break expectations. We want stories with fascinating characters and forward-thinking ideas. We want to keep exploring and celebrating the joy of storytelling.

If you want to help us and all the authors and artists that are part of our projects, please leave a review for this book! Every single review will help this title get noticed by someone who might not have seen it otherwise.

And stay tuned because we've got more coming . . .

OUR BOOKS

The Hole Behind Midnight, by Clinton J. Boomer
Crooked, by Richard Pett
Scourge of the Realm, by Erik Scott de Bie
Izanami's Choice, by Adam Heine
Pretty Marys All in a Row, by Gwendolyn Kiste
The Great Faerie Strike, by Spencer Ellsworth
Catfish Lullaby, by A.C. Wise
Busted Synapses, by Erica L. Satifka
Boneset & Feathers, by Gwendolyn Kiste
Alphabet of Lightning, by Edward Morris
The Obsecration, by Matthew M. Bartlett

COLLECTIONS

Royden Poole's Field Guide to the 25th Hour, by Clinton J. Boomer
Team Murderhobo: Assemble, by Clinton J. Boomer

ANTHOLOGIES
(edited by Scott Gable & C. Dombrowski)
By Faerie Light: Tales of the Fair Folk
Ghost in the Cogs: Steam-Powered Ghost Stories
Tomorrow's Cthulhu: Stories at the Dawn of Posthumanity
Ride the Star Wind: Cthulhu, Space Opera, and the Cosmic Weird
Welcome to Miskatonic University: Fantastically Weird Tales of Campus Life
It Came from Miskatonic University: Weirdly Fantastical Tales of Campus Life
Nowhereville: Weird Is Other People
Cooties Shot Required: There Are Things You Must Know
Whether Change: The Revolution Will Be Weird

Stay weird.
Read books.
Repeat.

brokeneyebooks.com
twitter.com/brokeneyebooks
facebook.com/brokeneyebooks
instagram.com/brokeneyebooks

BROKEN
eye
BOOKS